THE WORLD'S WORST CHILDREN 1

David Walliams

THE WORLD'S WORST CHILDREN 1

ILLUSTRATED BY *Tony Ross*

HarperCollins *Children's Books*

DAVID WALLIAMS

TONY ROSS

For
Tom & George,
two of the World's
Best Children
D.W.

For
Wendy,
& the Savannahs
T.R.

First published in the United Kingdom by
HarperCollins *Children's Books* in 2016
First published in this revised paperback edition in 2023
HarperCollins *Children's Books* is a division of
HarperCollins*Publishers* Ltd.
1 London Bridge Street, London SE1 9GF
www.harpercollins.co.uk
HarperCollins*Publishers*,
Macken House, 39/40 Mayor Street Upper,
Dublin 1, D01 C9W8, Ireland
1

David Walliams and Tony Ross assert the moral right
to be identified as the author and illustrator of the
work respectively.
Printed and bound in the UK using 100% renewable
electricity at CPI Group (UK) Ltd

Find out more about HarperCollins and the
environment at
www.harpercollins.co.uk/green

THANK YOUS

I would like to thank...

Tony Ross, *illustrator* – who, aged 6, filled a tin with tadpoles, left it in his grandmother's bedroom and forgot about it... until, several weeks later, his grandmother's screams reminded him as dozens of frogs hopped across her bed!

Ann-Janine Murtagh, *my publisher* – who as a little girl refused to go to sleep each night until every one of her 6 big sisters and brothers had told her a story – often making bedtime well past midnight!

Charlie Redmayne, *CEO* – who let his little sister take the blame for stealing a packet of jelly from the kitchen when in fact it was him – he never admitted the truth. Until now.

Paul Stevens, *my literary agent* – who as a little boy cut a hole in his dad's best suit jacket.

Ruth Alltimes, *my editor* – who, aged 5, poured a jug of orange squash over her little sister's head.

Rachel Denwood, *Publishing and Creative Director* – who, aged 6, decided to see how many peas she could put up her nose.

Sally Griffin, *Designer* – who, aged 7, picked ALL her mum's daffodils to sell in her 'flower shop'.

Anna Lubecka, *Designer* – who as a young girl cut off all of her hair with nail scissors.

Nia Roberts, *Art Director* – who, aged 6, painted over her parents' wedding photos with red nail varnish.

Kate Clarke, *my cover designer* – who as a young child cut up her mum's favourite – and very expensive – scarf, to use in a collage she was working on.

Geraldine Stroud, *PR Director* – who as a toddler mixed the contents of her mum's dressing table into a cake-shaped, perfumed mulch and spread it all over the house.

Sam White, *my publicist* – who as a small child did a wee in her mum's bed and didn't tell her.

Nicola Way, *Marketing Director* – who, aged 5, kidnapped her little brother and the dog and went on the run for a whole hour!

Alison Ruane, *Brand Director* – who, aged 10, would bake chilli powder scones and make her little brothers eat them.

Georgia Monroe, *Desk Editor* – who as a toddler splattered nappy cream all over her bedroom when she was meant to be having a nap!

Tanya Brennand-Roper, *my audio editor* – who as a young child collected worms from the garden and put them in the kitchen so her mum would scream!

David Walliams

INTRODUCTION

by Raj, a newsagent.

Please, please, please, a thousand pleases, and yet one more please

DO NOT READ THIS BOOK!

If you have already bought it, destroy it. If you are browsing through it in your local librarium, take it outside, tear it up, stamp on it, tear it up again just to be sure and then bury the pieces DEEP underground. To be totally safe.

This AWFUL book, and it is awful, especially the speling, will have a very bad influence on young minds. It will give children lots and lots of ideas about how to be even naughtier than they already are, and some of them are already EXTREMELY naughty. It is an outrage and I for one will be calling for this book to be banned. Mr Wallybottom (or whatever his stupid made-up name is) should be ashamed of himself.

Why can't the oversized BUFFOON who looks like a cupboard in a suit write a nice book about nice children who do nice things? Why not write a story about a little girl who is kind to a kitten? Or a tale about a nice boy who helps an injured butterfly cross a busy road? Or a story about two children who go to a meadow and pick wild flowers for their mummy who is very ill with a slight headache?

It could be called

THE WORLD'S NICEST, KINDEST, BESTEST, MOST LOVELIEST CHILDREN IN THE WHOLE WORLD.

But no.

Instead we get a BUCKETLOAD of stories about children with bottoms that don't stop blowing off, children who teach their nits to do terrible things and children who won't stop picking their noses until they create the world's largest bogey.

These are children who I would NEVER ever allow in my newsagent's shop, which I am extremely proud to say was recently voted best newsagent in the parade.*

* RAJ'S NEWSAGENT IS CURRENTLY THE ONLY NEWSAGENT IN THE PARADE. SAYING THAT, MY SHOP DID COME SECOND LAST YEAR IN A POLL OF BEST NEWSAGENTS. THE LAUNDERETTE CAME FIRST.

I would never let the frankly APPALLING children featured in this book take advantage of the very special offers in my shop, such as my **103 sherbert fountains for the price of 102,** or **buy your own bodyweight in mints, get one mint free. Hurry while stocks last!** **

** STOCKS HAVE GONE.

What's worst of all is that I am hardly in this book. It's an insult! I am by far the most cleverest and handsomest character that ever came out of **Mr Wallywilly's** dark and troubled mind! Yet I was only asked to contribute an introduction, and was under strict instructions that said introduction be no longer than two pages. Two pages!

How dare **Mr Willywillybumbum?** Surely I, the

GREAT RAJ OF RAJ'S NEWSAGEN

CONTENTS

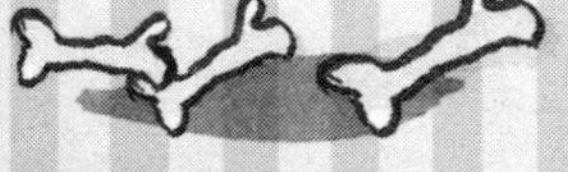

Dribbling
DREW

DRIBBLE OF DROOL

POOL OF DROOL

DAMP SHOES AND SOCKS
FROM THE POOL OF DROOL

Dribbling
DREW

ONCE UPON A TIME there was a boy named Drew.
Drew **dribbled** a lot. This wasn't just normal everyday
dribbling, the odd globule of gob gloop running
down your chin. Oh no, this was dribbling on an
INDUSTRIAL SCALE. Here was a boy who
could dribble litre upon litre of dribble a day.

Now you may wonder why **Dribbling Drew** dribbled so much. Well, it was because he was an incredibly lazy individual. If he could, he would sleep **24 hours a day, 7 days a week, 365 days a year**.

And, as Drew snoozed, he drooled.

"**ZZZZZZz.**"

PLOP!

went the drool as it   "**ZZZZZZZZZz.**"
landed on the floor.   PLOP!

On school mornings, the boy would have to be dragged out of bed by his feet. If he had his way, Drew would be wheeled to school every morning in his bed. And, as soon as he arrived at school, he would go straight back to sleep.

"**ZZZZZZz.**"

PLOP!   "**ZZZZZZZZZZZZZz.**"
              PLOP!

Drew liked nothing more than having a nice long snooze during his lessons. He had even been known to take a sleeping bag into school. That way he could doze through every single subject.

PE was a hard one to sleep through, but Drew found a way. For example, during football matches he would ask to be in goal and then climb up on to the net and have a nap. If any of the kids scored a goal, he would moan if they celebrated too loudly and woke him up.

Because Drew slept through every lesson, he always found himself bottom of the class.

When Drew snoozed in lessons, he would dribble all over his desk.

"ZZZZZZz."

PLOP!

"ZZZZZZZZZZZZzz."

PLOP!

"ZZZZZZZZZZZZZZZZZZZZZZZzz."

PLOP!

The dribble would $^t r_i c_k l_e$ down to the floor, where a large puddle of drool would collect. If the lesson was DREADED double history, the dribble would end up as something of a pool.

No one knew quite what was in Drew's dribble. It was transparent like water, but thick and sticky like glue.

One time his history teacher, Miss Past, ran over to Drew's desk to **shout** at him for falling asleep in class again. The unfortunate lady **slipped** on the **dribble**, shot across the floor and flew straight out of the **window**. "AAARRRGGGHH!"

She was found upside down in a nearby hedgerow with her tweed skirt over her head, her BIG frilly **knickers** flapping in the wind.

The day our story starts, there was a school trip to the

· NATURAL HISTORY MUSEUM ·

This was a wondrous place, full of all sorts of treasures from Moon rock to dinosaur skeletons. The museum even housed a life-sized cast of a blue whale.

As Drew's class pulled up outside the museum in the school coach, Mr Numbings, the science teacher, handed out his dreaded worksheets. "Now listen carefully, children. On these worksheets I want you to make a list of all the exhibits you see in the museum today!"

"Do we have to, sir?" moaned **Dribbling Drew**, stifling a yawn. Dozing on the coach for an hour had tired the boy out and now he was ready for bed. A pool of drool had collected at his feet.

"Yes, Drew, we do have to!" yelled the teacher. "And I want you to stay awake during this visit!" Mr Numbings turned back to the rest of the class. "Now, everyone, the pupil who writes down the most exhibits will come TOP of the class. So keep looking and listening the whole time. Right, out you get!"

As they walked in through the museum's giant wooden doors, all the children marvelled at the huge skeleton of a **diplodocus**, which took pride of place in the great hall. But Drew simply YAWNED.

Then he broke away from his teacher and classmates and found a nice quiet place to nap. It was on top of a glass case housing a stuffed dodo, a bird that had become extinct centuries before. No one would disturb him up there.

Drew climbed up, using a **stuffed giraffe** as a ladder.

He lay down and closed his eyes. Then the boy slept and slept and slept.

And **dribbled** and **dribbled** and **dribbled**.

The boy could sleep absolutely anywhere.
Standing up during a rock concert,
hanging N⅄Oᗡ ƎᗡISᗡ∩ from
a tree, even on a rollercoaster
as everyone around him screamed.

This particular day, Drew slept for
so long that he was still asleep when the
• NATURAL HISTORY MUSEUM • was locked up for the
night. Without anyone realising, he was still there when
all the lights were turned off.

All night Drew slept and, as he slept, he **dribbled**.

"ZZZZZZZZZZZZZZ."

PLOP!

"ZZZZZZZZZZZZZZZZZZZZZZZZ."

PLOP!

"ZZZZZZZZZZZZZZZzzzzzzzzz."

PLOP!

Drew **dribbled** and **dribbled** and **dribbled**.
Then he **dribbled** some more. The spot of drool beneath
him spread into a puddle. Soon it was a lake of
spittle. By dawn, Drew's sea of **dribble** had filled
the entire • NATURAL HISTORY MUSEUM • .

In the morning, Winston, the burly security guard, arrived bright and early to unlock the doors and open the museum as he did every day. However, this was no ordinary day. The first thing Winston noticed was a transparent fluid oozing underneath the doors.

"That's very strange," he thought out loud. "Maybe one of the daft old professors has left a tap running."

Next, the security guard dipped the toe of his boot into the liquid, and realised it couldn't be water from a leaky pipe. Whatever this was, it was **THICK** and **STICKY**.

Worried that the museum might have been flooded, Winston flung open the giant wooden doors as fast as he could.

Nothing could have prepared Winston for what happened next...

WHOOSH!

A **TIDAL** wave of *drool* washed him CLEAN off his **feet** and he found himself travelling at S P E E D down the street.

"**WAAAH!**" the big man screamed like a baby.

Closely behind the security guard floated some of the biggest exhibits from the museum. A stuffed polar bear, the life-sized cast of the blue whale, even the **diplodocus skeleton**.

They all bobbed along the streets of London on this rushing river of **dribble**.

Atop the glass case that housed the dodo was Drew. In all the commotion, he had finally woken up from his long sleep. As he floated down the road, the flood of his own spittle destroyed everything in its path.

Cars, lorries and even buses were swept off the ground and began bobbing along on the colossal ooze of drool.

Drew leaped off the glass case on to the roof of a nearby building.

From that safe place he watched more of the exhibits from the museum pass by.

Giant birds' eggs,

a stuffed gorilla,

a model of an elephant.

The boy reached into his blazer pocket. He still had the worksheet his teacher, Mr Numbings, had given him at the start of the school trip. Drew made a note of everything he saw.

Every single exhibit from the museum floated past, and he wrote them all down.

"**Mars rock,**

a Neanderthal skull,

a marble statue of Charles Darwin,

 **a giant squid,**

a stuffed vulture,

an earthquake machine,

a model T-Rex..."

The list went ON and ON.

"**A sea horse pickled in a jar,**

a model volcano,

a fossil of a prehistoric fish,

a spacesuit,

a stuffed giraffe,

an old lady clinging on to her shopper –

hang on, that's a real old lady –

a model of a woolly mammoth..."

To his credit, **Dribbling Drew** spent hours listing everything he saw as the gushing river of drool swept all the museum's precious exhibits out to sea.

The next day in class Drew proudly handed in his worksheet to Mr Numbings. Aside from a few spots of dribble, it was perfect. After looking through all of his pupils' work, the science teacher announced the results.

"I can reveal that the winner, with one hundred per cent, is Drew!" said Mr Numbings.

The boy was top of the class for the very first time in his life.

Before he was promptly expelled!

As a punishment for destroying everything in the
• NATURAL HISTORY MUSEUM • , Drew was put to work
there. His job was to reassemble the **diplodocus skeleton**
that had been recovered from the bottom of the sea.
He was not to stop until this giant jigsaw was finished.

Dribbling Drew didn't get any sleep

for the next

ten

years.

THIS STORY
IS FAR TOO
SOGGY!

BERTHA
the Blubberer

BERTHA WAS A BLUBBERER. She would sob. She would howl. She would bawl. The little girl was only eight years old, but she must have spent seven of them **blubbering**.

Anything and EVERYTHING would set her off.

Loud noise
Silence
Bright lights
The dark
Small dogs
Large dogs
Medium-sized dogs
Rodents of any kind
Red socks
Frogs
Toads
Tadpoles especially
Bouncing balls
Fireworks
Dust
The heat
The cold
Ducks, geese and swans
Orange juice with bits in
Burnt toast
Kettles
Stickers
Wet grass

Park benches
Men with tattoos
Low-flying aircraft
The colour purple
Cat hair
Rain
Waterslides
Mud
Anything made of plastic
Christmas crackers
The raisins in raisin biscuits
Bouncy castles
Smells of any kind,
  even nice ones
Clouds
Moustaches
Vegetables
Burps
Monobrows
Nostril hair
Ear hair
Anyone in a hat

The little girl had a younger brother called William. From the day he was born Bertha was beastly to him. She hated having to share her parents' attention. Then one day Bertha discovered a wonderful thing. She could cry and blame it all on her little brother. And the more she cried, the more attention SHE got.

So the girl thought up more and more wicked plans to make William look horrid. Bertha's favourite ploy was to cry and cry and cry alone in her bedroom, pretending her brother had hurt her. When Mother bounded up the stairs to see what was wrong, Bertha would blub through a river of tears, "Mama, it was William! He pinched me! William pinched me, hard, on the arm!"

Sometimes she would elaborate on the lie by actually pinching herself. Bertha would then offer up the very tiny red BLOTCH on her arm as evidence of her brother's beastliness.

"WAHAHAHAHAHAHAHAHAHAHAHAHAHAH

she would wail.

Then Mother would burst into her son's room next door to confront the boy. Young William was usually reading or playing quietly with his earplugs in. He had endured a lifetime of bawling, and had therefore fashioned earplugs out of **marshmallows** so he could get on with things in peace.

"Why did you pinch your darling sister?" Mother would demand.

"What?" William would reply. It was hard to hear with **marshmallows** in his ears.

"And why have you got **marshmallows** in your ears?"

William would take out the **marshmallows** and protest his innocence.

"I haven't touched her, Mother," the boy would plead. "I have been reading in my room the whole time!"

HAHAHAHAHA!"

"A likely story!" Mother would declare. "No **pudding** for you after dinner tonight!"

"But…!"

"No **pudding** for a week!"

"But…!" "No **pudding** for a month!"

Eventually the boy would fall silent. He liked **pudding**. But not as much as his sister. The little girl loved **pudding**. Even more than she loved crying.

Once, at the local bakery, she even offered to swap her brother for a slice of chocolate fudge cake. It was a large slice, but still…

And, if there was no **pudding** for William, Bertha would be allowed to eat his. DOUBLE **pudding!** All Bertha had to do was roll around on her bed and **blubber**.

On the day our story begins, the two children were left alone inside the house. Mother was in the garden, tending to her beloved roses as Father mowed the lawn.

Spotting that her parents were outside, a fiendish scheme crossed Bertha's mind. It was her most devilish plot yet, breathtakingly simple and all the more brilliant for it. The plan was this: Bertha would pull out a clump of her hair and then bawl the house down. When Mother and Father came running, the finger of blame would be pointed at poor William. Pulling out a clump of hair would appear to be William's worst crime yet. It trumped pinching, **PRODDING**, poking, **biting**, **dead arms** and **DEAD LEGS**. He would surely be packed straight off to an orphanage. And Bertha would have DOUBLE **pudding** – maybe even TRIPLE **pudding** – every night for the rest of her life.

It was glorious. **Pudding,** **pudding** and more **pudding!**

The **wicked** little girl tiptoed over to her brother's room to check he was there. Indeed he was, quietly getting on with his homework with his **marshmallow** earplugs in as usual.

Next Bertha sneaked back to her room. She looked at herself in the mirror and began phase one of her plan. She reached up to her head and grabbed a clump of hair. Shutting her eyes, she yanked as hard as she could. Bertha didn't need to pretend to cry. The pain was so intense that she couldn't help but yell.

"WAHAHAHAHAHAHAHAHAHAHAHAHAHAHAHAHA"

She examined the strands of her hair in her hand and the bald spot she had made on her head. It was about the size of a ping-pong ball. Bertha then put her ear to her bedroom door, to see if her parents were on their way. Strangely they were not.

So Bertha did it again.

"WAHAHAHAHAHAHAHAHAHAHAHAHAHAHAHAHAHAHAHAHAHAHAHAHAHAHAH!!!"

This time she yanked even more hair from her head.

Now there was another bald spot. This one was the size of a TENNIS ball. Still no one came running.

So Bertha did it again.

"WAHAHAHAHA!"

And again.

"WAHAHA!!"

And again.

"WAHAHAHA

HAHAHAHAHA

HAHAHAHAHA

HAHAHAHA

HAHAHAHA

HAHAHAHA
HAHAHAHAHA
HAHAHAHAHA
HAHAHA
HAHAHA
HAHAHA
HAHAHA
HAHAHA
HAHA!!!"

The pain was so extreme that Bertha's eyes were now stinging with tears. She could barely see what she was doing any more.

Yet still the girl

yanked out

more and

more

of her hair.

Eventually, wiping the tears from her face, she stared in the mirror. Bertha was now completely bald, except for one lonely strand of hair on the top of her head.

Just then she heard a noise. Bertha's eyes darted to her bedroom door. To her horror, her mother, father and brother were all looking at her through the door-crack.

Bertha stared at them for a moment and they stared back at her.

How was she going to explain this?

Bertha didn't know what to do, so she did what she always did. The girl screwed up her face, and began bawling.

"WAHAHAHAHAHA!"

It never failed.

"WAHAHAHAHAHAHAHA!"

Except THIS time.

"What on earth are you crying for?" demanded Father.

"Because, Mama and Papa, that beastly brother of mine pulled out ALL of my hair!" replied the girl through her theatrical sobs.

William couldn't help but *smirk* at the sight of his wicked sister, who had at last been well and truly BUSTED!

"Actually, you've still got one hair sticking out of the top of your head!" proclaimed the boy.

Bertha examined herself in the mirror again. It did look rather strange having just the one lonely strand, so she plucked it out between her fingers. "WAHAHAHAHAHAHAHAHAHA!"

"That can't have hurt," protested William. "It was just one little hair."

Bertha was becoming desperate now.

"B-b-but YOU pulled out all the others, William, you evil little WRETCH!"

"We have been standing here for the last few minutes, young lady," began Mother.

"We saw the **whole** thing," added Father.

The **smuggest** grin spread across William's already smug face.

"B-b-but..." protested Bertha.

"No doubt you have been doing this all along!" accused Mother.

"B-b-b-b-but..."

"No **pudding** for you, young lady..." declared Father.

Bertha **stopped** protesting for a moment. The punishment didn't seem so bad. Missing **one pudding**. She had a stash of chocolate under her bed anyway. The girl gave her brother a self-satisfied look. Then, like a prizefighter, Mother delivered the **knockout** blow.

"...**EVER** AGAIN!"

Bertha froze. This was worse than having no hair. No puddings! But Bertha loved **puddings**. If she could, she would only eat **puddings, puddings, puddings**.

How could anyone live without:

cake

and

ice cream

and

meringues and cream

and

sponge cake

and

and

ETON MESS

custard tarts

and

and

treacle sponge

French fancies

and

apple crumble and custard

and

jelly

and

spotted dick

and

cupcakes

and

sticky toffee pudding

JAM ROLY-POLY

and

and

Chocolate mousse

trifle?

and

All preferably eaten
in ONE sitting.

brandy snaps

"Really, Mama?" pleaded the girl. "This can't be true. No **puddings** forever?"

"Forever and ever and ever," replied Mother, who was mightily cross that her daughter had fooled her for so long.

Now every night Bertha would have to watch her brother across the dinner table, savouring every last morsel of not only his delicious **pudding**, but what would have been Bertha's too.

DOUBLE pudding!

Most evenings Mother would give William her own pudding as well, to make up for his harsh treatment over the years.

TRIPLE pudding!

Often the boy would be allowed to eat his father's **pudding** too.

QUADRUPLE pudding!

It was torture for the girl to watch her brother eat
all her favourite pudding night after night after night
while she had not a crumb of one.

Bakewell tart,

Arctic roll,

Eton mess;

William would lick
the bowls clean!

To make matters worse, under the table the boy would
pinch his sister's leg as he scoffed away.

"WAHAHAHAHAHAHAHAHAHAHAHAHAHAHA!!!!"

"He pinched me!" Bertha would cry.

Nobody ever believed her.

BERTHA
THE BLUBBERER

had **blubbered**

one too many **blubbers**.

MY EARS HURT!

NIGEL
Nit-Boy

NITS ARE ITCHY. Nits are scratchy. Nits are scritchy. Nits are a NUISANCE.

Not for Nigel. Nigel was a boy who could never have enough nits. He wanted his hair **crawling** with them.

Our tale begins on the morning that Nigel woke up to discover he had a nit living in his hair. Most of us would be appalled and immediately try to evict the nit.

Not Nigel. He was delighted.

The boy called this nit MR HENDERSON. Nigel didn't have a dog or a cat or a hamster, so he treated his nit like a pet. He made sure he never combed his hair (nits hate combs). Soon Nigel's hair was *wild* and **frizzy**, like a great big bush.

A jungle paradise for nits.

BEFORE

AFTER

Nigel fed Mr Henderson titbits of dandruff (nits love dandruff) in the hope of training him up to do tricks, like leaping from one side of Nigel's head to the other.

Soon afterwards, Nigel heard of another child at school who had nits. Her name was Tina Ting. Nigel wanted Tina's nits more than anything in the world. He wanted nits, nits and more nits! At break-time Nigel chased the poor girl round the playground.

"What do you want?" cried Tina tearfully. "I am not playing 'it'!"

"I want your **nits!**" replied the boy.

"My nits? You are **nuts!**" yelled the girl.

"Yes, I am **NUTS** for **nits!**" said Nigel.

The boy tripped over a skateboard and flew through the air towards her.

CLONK! Their heads bashed and, in an instant, Tina's nits crawled over to Nigel's head...

A little dazed, the boy was nonetheless happy. Now Mr Henderson had some company.

The next day Nigel heard of a boy in school who had nits: Colin Clont. Nigel wanted those nits so **badly**. So he chased Colin down the corridor and cornered him in the toilets.

NIGEL NIT-BOY

The trembling boy locked himself in a cubicle, but Nigel would not give up. He climbed over the top of the next cubicle and dangled upside down from the ceiling. Nigel's and Colin's heads knocked together.

Once again the nits sprang across to Nigel's head. **BONK!**

Even the school cat was not safe from Nigel's advances. When Nigel was told that Minky the cat also had nits, he pursued the poor creature across the football field. Once he had caught the cat, he Sellotaped it to his head. It looked like a very unconvincing wig.

Still, one by one the cat's nits bounded on to Nigel's head.

Soon Nigel had so many nits that even his nits had nits. He stopped counting them at a million and three.

*　*　*

Now you may be wondering why Nigel wanted a headful of nits. Please let me explain. Ever since he was a toddler, Nigel had spent his days reading comics. The boy was short for his age (if you don't count the wild bush of hair on top of his head) and he wanted to be strong and POWERFUL like the characters in his comics. However, Nigel had had a very normal upbringing. He'd not been lucky enough to have been

bitten by a **RADIOACTIVE SPIDER**,

or come from a **VIKING PLANET**,

or fallen down a well of **BATS**.

Besides, he found superheroes a bit boring. They were always doing good. The SUPERVILLAINS were so much more thrilling. Before long, naughty Nigel had a plan.

One morning as the boy was standing in the bathroom cleaning his teeth, he looked at himself in the mirror. His hair was now not so much a bush, more of a hedgerow. Nigel could not remember the last time he had either cut or combed it.

Buzzing in and out of this hedgerow of hair were billions of nits, forming a dark cloud around him.

"The day has finally come. My nit-based superpower is ready! From this day on the world will know me only as...

NIT-BOY!"

Best of all, the name hadn't already been taken.

So now that Nigel had all his nits, he went about getting a costume made. Fortunately, the boy's Auntie Pat was quite good at sewing and put together a SUPERVILLAIN costume for her nephew in no time.

Nigel wore...

a cape fashioned from one of his mum's skirts

the NB logo for 'Nit-Boy' sewn by Auntie Pat

his dad's old Y-fronts

his nana's tights

Wellington boots

Nigel had his superpower.

He had his name.

His costume was on.

He was **NIT-BOY!**

At once he began his SUPERVILLAINY.

The next morning he strode into school, his cape flapping in the wind. First, Nigel vowed to get revenge on his geography teacher, Mr Drumhum. Nigel found geography boring and spent most of his lessons reading comic books. Mr Drumhum had given the boy detention after detention. Now **NIT-BOY** stood at the door to the classroom. Initially there were hoots of laughter from the other children. What with his costume and shrubland of hair, the would-be SUPERVILLAIN did look quite a sight. **"HA HA HA!"**

However, the laughter turned to silent awe as **NIT-BOY** called out his first command. **"NITS! SWARM!"**

The billions of nits that were whirling round his head formed a black mass next to him.

"Nigel, what on earth do you think you are doing?" demanded Mr Drumhum.

"NITS! ATTACK!"

shouted the boy.

They swarmed the geography teacher, nipping him all over with their tiny lice claws.

"**Argh!**" screamed Mr Drumhum as he raced out of the classroom.

All his pupils pressed their faces up against the windows to watch their teacher.

The man was trying desperately to fend off the nits. He was hopping and spinning and slapping himself as

he sped across the playing field towards the school pond. Mr Drumhum then leaped in with a giant SPLOSH

He finally had some relief from the nit nips.

Though now he was submerged in green water with a fat frog sitting on his head.

NIT-BOY smiled to himself.

This was going to be fun.

Next he marched across the playground to the dining hall. The dinner lady, Mrs Droop, was something of a dragon. Boiled broccoli was her signature dish. Whatever you chose, even jam roly-poly and custard, Mrs Droop would spoon heaps of her green watery mush on top. Then she would stalk up and down the dining tables, twirling her ladle like a baton, threatening to rap the knuckles of anyone who didn't eat up every last mouthful.

Nigel hated broccoli. If Superman feared Kryptonite, **NIT-BOY** was terrified of broccoli. Now he was to have his revenge on the woman who had made him eat a mountain of it.

"Nigel…" she purred as he strode in. "Why have you got your pants on over your trousers? Ha ha ha!"

Mrs Droop's smile was wiped off her face as soon as **NIT-BOY** shouted out his next command.

"NITS! TO THE BROCCOLI!"

"I am not having your blasted head lice messing with my delicious broccoli!" protested the dinner lady.

Too late. The nits had swarmed into a whirling tornado. Mrs Droop stood open-mouthed in shock as this twisting vortex spun over to her precious trays of broccoli. Then the tornado started firing the damp, limp vegetable straight at Mrs Droop.

SPLAT!

SPLAT!

SPLAT!

Soggy floret after soggy floret splattered across the woman's face until Mrs Droop was a damp, green, vegetably mess.

Now **NIT-BOY** was ready to have his revenge on his headmaster. The elderly Mr Sourchops had suspended Nigel from school after his tenth detention for reading comic books in lessons. The headmaster was a small and timid man, so **NIT-BOY** thought he would frighten him. Nigel stood in the playground just below the window of the headmaster's office. He closed his eyes in concentration.

"NITS! SHAPE-SHIFT!" he ordered.

Slowly the tiny insects swarmed together into the shape of a giant supernit. They were able to read their master's mind. As the boy kept his eyes tightly shut, a look of intense concentration on his face, the giant nit-shape surged upwards to the headmaster's window. It banged on the glass with its huge claw.

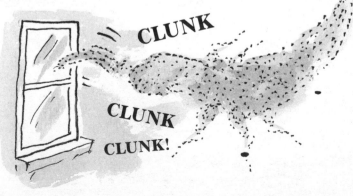

CLUNK

CLUNK

CLUNK!

Mr Sourchops swivelled round in his chair and shrieked.

"NOOOOOOOOO!"

The giant nit bashed its great head against
the window, breaking the glass. CRACK!

"HELP!" screamed the headmaster as he dashed out of
his office. Running into the playground, Mr Sourchops
spotted a wheelie bin.

Checking behind himself all the time for the giant
supernit, the old man pushed the bin as hard as he
could before leaping into it as it was speeding away.

Finally NIT-BOY opened his eyes and watched in
glee as his headmaster trundled across the
playground in the bin.

It bashed into a low wall...

CLANG!

...sending the old man flying through the air straight into a tree trunk.

CLUNK!

The nits swarmed back to their master's head as Nigel strode out of the school gates.

There was plenty more SUPERVILLAINY to be done.

Not long after, **NIT-BOY** arrived in the market square, which was teeming with bargain-hunters. Using his nits Nigel spelled out the letters of a very rude word in the sky.

bottoms

Next **NIT-BOY** turned his attention to the local toyshop. The SUPERVILLAIN ordered his nits to steal every single item in the store, including the till.

The shop owner chased the boy down the street, but he was whacked over the head by the nits with one of his own giant teddy bears.

Yet there was still more chaos and destruction to come.

Suddenly lights flashed and a siren wailed. The police had been sent to stop Nigel from creating further mayhem. But **NIT-BOY** ordered his nits to attack the police car and they swarmed on to its windscreen. The glass became so thick with nits that the policeman crashed straight into the window of an optician's.

SMASH!

OPTICIAN

NOW YOU CAN SEE WHERE YOU ARE GOING!

Nothing could stop **NIT-BOY** now. He felt invincible. Soon the whole world would kneel before him.

ALL HAIL, **NIT-BOY!**

Later that night, Nigel had put on his pyjamas and was lying in bed. Even SUPERVILLAINS need their sleep. The boy was dreaming up the next day's evil schemes.

However, outside in the street stood a throng of townsfolk, armed not with flaming torches and pitchforks, as is the tradition with angry mobs, but with an array of combs. NIT-BOY had to be robbed of his powers. And there was only one way to do that.

They began to chant,

"COMB HIS HAIR! COMB HIS HAIR!"

The chant became louder and louder as the mob grew angrier and angrier.

Nigel leaped from his bed and peeked out of his window. Looking down, he saw more and more people rushing out of their houses to join the horde.

In a swirling *whirl* of nits, Nigel changed out of his pyjamas to become... **NIT-BOY!**

He marched outside and approached the mob. With his Wellington boots on and his cape (which was really one of his mum's old skirts) flapping in the wind, **NIT-BOY** felt ready to take on the world.

His millions of nits had now multiplied into billions or maybe even trillions.*

They buzzed round the boy's head, blacking out the scattering of stars in the night sky.

*It would be hard to give you an exact number because nits won't stay still, making counting them IMPOSSIBLE.

- 72 -

"THERE HE IS!" shouted someone.

"IT'S **NIT-BOY!** "

"GET HIM!"

The mob surged forwards, brandishing their combs. The old lady who had fainted in the market square was holding a large bottle of anti-nit shampoo called **Nit-Blitz**. On the label it said:

The sworn enemy of the **NIT!** *This HIGHLY TOXIC and foul-smelling shampoo is poisonous to all known nits. It is GUARANTEED to kill nits until they are totally and utterly COMPLETELY* **DEAD!**

Unable to contain her anger a moment longer, the old lady hurled the bottle at Nigel. It bounced off his hair and hit her on the head, knocking her out cold.

The boy still stood his ground. Once again he
commanded his nits.

"NITS! LIFT!"

The nits swooped downwards to create a hoverboard
under their master's feet. Then they lifted him off the
ground with laughable ease.

The crowd gasped in shock. This SUPERVILLAIN
could actually fly!

The boy zoomed through the night sky, performing an impressive loop the loop, before hovering over the mob.

"NOW GO BACK TO YOUR HOMES OR YOU WILL FEEL THE FULL FORCE OF *NIT-BOY!*"

The townsfolk began muttering to each other dejectedly. They knew they were beaten, yet still no one moved.

"DISPERSE!" *NIT-BOY* ordered the crowd.

But his nits must have thought he was talking to them. Nits are not known for their intelligence. As far as I know, no nit has performed brain surgery or been involved in rocket science. So the nits...

...D I S P E R S E D.

Led by Mr Henderson,

they all buzzed off in different directions,

disappearing

into the sky.

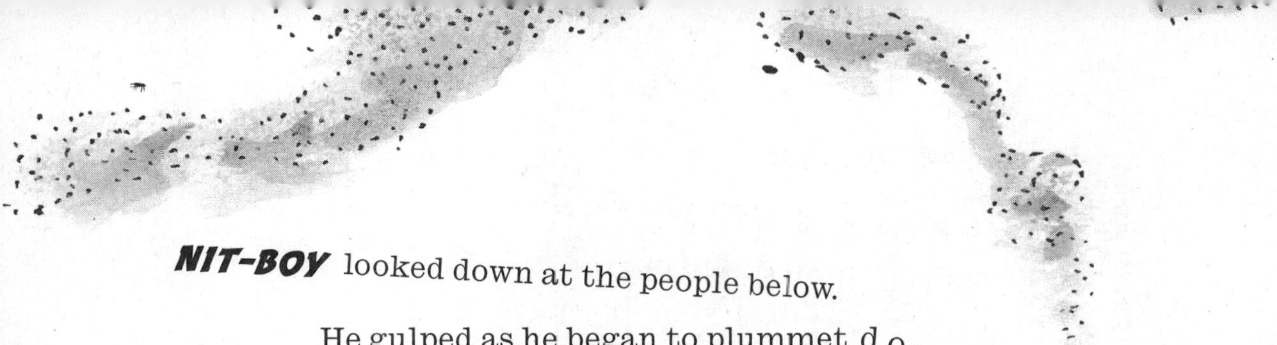

NIT-BOY looked down at the people below.

He gulped as he began to plummet d o w n
w
a
r
d
s.

He tumbled through

the air, desperately

flapping his arms.

"HELP!"

The crowd surged out of the way, and Nigel landed headfirst on the pavement. Fortunately, such was the volume of hair on his head that he survived the fall without injury.

"GRAB HIM!"

shouted someone.

Nigel was carted off to the local hairdresser's where his hair was washed with **Nit-Blitz** shampoo and he was given a very sensible short back and sides.

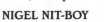
All remaining nits or nit eggs were combed out of Nigel's hair and he had to make a promise in front of the whole town.

"I solemnly swear never, ever to become **NIT-BOY** again."

You might be surprised to learn that, even though he was one of the world's worst children, Nigel kept his promise. **NIT-BOY** was never seen again.

However, some time later Nigel came up with another SUPERVILLAIN to be.

From now on he would be known as...

VERRUCA-BOY!*

A SUPERVILLAIN who refused to wear a plastic sock at the swimming pool, thereby unleashing a plague of **verrucas** on the world.

And the best part was that Nigel could reuse the cape that was really his mum's old **skirt**.

*Again, fortunately the name had **not** already been taken.

Miss PETULA
Perpetual-Motion

THIS IS THE STORY OF A GIRL who would **not** sit still.
Miss Petula Perpetual-Motion was forever in motion.
Whether she was in a lesson, in church or even playing
Musical Statues, some part of her would always be
moving. It might be her foot, or her arm, or even her
entire body.

It would start with

a little wiggle, then

become a waggle,

before turning

into a jiggle and

progressing to a JOGGLE.

Next she would be cartwheeling across the room, creating pandemonium wherever she went.

Petula was even in motion as she slept. Sometimes the other girls at her posh boarding school, *Modesty Place*, would hear a noise in the dead of night. They would peek out from under their bedcovers and see Petula ballet-dancing across the dormitory with her eyes closed.

One day, Petula's rather grand headmistress announced that the girls of *Modesty Place* were to go on an awfully special trip.

"Quiet, girls!" ordered the lady as she stood on stage at assembly. Miss Prigg's grey hair was styled in a magnificent bouffant hairdo and a pair of half-moon spectacles hung from her neck on a gold chain. If she was about to tell someone off (which was often), the spectacles would be lifted up to her eyes so she could stare her victim down and give them the *willies*.

"Now, girls, we are going to take a school trip to somewhere I – your beloved headmistress – have chosen myself. We are going to visit my favourite **PORCELAIN** museum. Needless to say, I expect you to be on your absolute best behaviour. I don't want any mishaps."

Suddenly all eyes were on Petula.

OH NO! thought the *good* girls sitting in the front row.

OH YES! thought the *bad* girls sitting in the back row.

To make matters worse (or better, depending on whether you were a good or bad girl), Petula was bouncing up and down on her seat like it was a space hopper.

BOING!
BOING!
BOING!

"**PORCELAIN** has long been a personal passion of mine," continued the headmistress, who loved making lengthy speeches. "Now I – your beloved headmistress – want to share that passion with you. This museum is the best in Europe. Every single piece on display is a priceless antique. There shall be no *'accidents'*. Do I make myself clear?"

There was a faint murmur from the pupils.

"I SAID DO I MAKE MYSELF **CLEAR?!**" she bellowed.

"**Yes,** Headmistress," chimed the girls in unison.

"Excellent! Now, *Miss Petula Perpetual-Motion*, I need to see you in my study right away."

The girl glowed as red as a tomato driving a fire engine. What had she done wrong now?

Surely the time when she accidentally spun backwards into the science block had been put behind her? Yes, the experiment taking place that day went badly wrong. Yes, there was still a huge hole in the floor where the acid burned through it. But Petula swore it was an accident.

Yes, her triple jump on sports day became an *octuple* jump (taking in eight different moves) and resulted in Petula karate-kicking the local mayor, sending him tumbling off the winners' podium.

But again the girl insisted it was an accident.

And yes, of course, who could forget the time at the school Christmas Carol Concert when Petula couldn't stand still in church, cartwheeled up the aisle and sent the vicar flying headfirst into the choir?

But these were all accidents.

It wasn't her fault she couldn't sit still.

Petula even had a note from her **mother** to prove it.

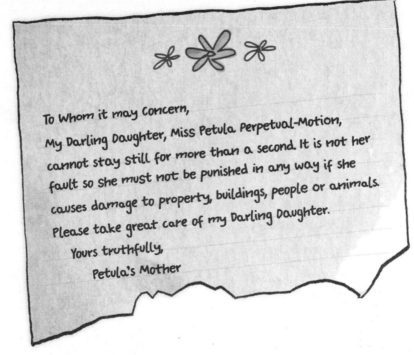

To Whom it may Concern,

My Darling Daughter, Miss Petula Perpetual-Motion, cannot stay still for more than a second. It is not her fault so she must not be punished in any way if she causes damage to property, buildings, people or animals. Please take great care of my Darling Daughter.

Yours truthfully,

Petula's Mother

With some trepidation, the girl knocked on the door of the headmistress's study.

KNOCK **KNOCK** KNOCK!

"Come!" barked the headmistress from inside.

KNOCK KNOCK KNOCK KNOCK KNOCK!

Petula's hand did not stop knocking.

"I SAID COME!" came an angry-sounding voice.

Still Petula couldn't stop her hand from knocking.

KNOCK KNOCK KNOCK KNOCK KNOCK KNOCK KNOCK KNOCK!

"Oh, for goodness' sake!" roared the headmistress.

Miss Prigg yanked open the door and Petula

KNOCK-KNOCK-KNOCKED the lady

slap-bang on her nose.

BOINK!

"Ow!"

"Sorry, Miss Prigg," replied the
girl with a hint of a smile.
It was amusing to see the
lady fuming.

"COME INTO MY STUDY
THIS INSTANT!"
ordered the headmistress.

Petula forward-rolled into the room, which Miss Prigg always had kept spotless. In fact an old cleaner was in there at that moment, busily polishing some school trophies on a table.

"You – out!" ordered the headmistress. Miss Prigg was curt to anyone she considered below her.

The cleaner picked up her dusters and shuffled towards the door.

"Quickly!" shouted Miss Prigg, and the poor old dear picked up her pace until at last she disappeared.

"Now take a seat, *Miss Petula Perpetual-Motion.*" said the headmistress.

Petula did just that. She took a seat, and **danced** round the study with it.

"I meant, sit down!" barked Miss Prigg.

The girl whisked and whirled the chair to the floor, and slowly lowered herself on to it.

As soon as her bottom touched the chair she felt an overwhelming urge to bounce up and down on it, so she did.

"Be still!" demanded Miss Prigg. But Petula continued to bounce up and down, the chair squeaking along rhythmically with her bounces.

BOUNCE
SQUEAK!

BOUNCE
SQUEAK!

BOUNCE
SQUEAK!

"Now, needless to say, I want you on your absolute best behaviour during the school trip."

"Of course, Miss Prigg. As if I would be anything else."

BOUNCE
SQUEAK!

BOUNCE
SQUEAK!

BOUNCE
SQUEAK!

The headmistress was not convinced. She lifted her half-moon spectacles up to her eyes and studied the girl.

"The truth is, you have left a trail of **destruction** behind you wherever you've been at ⌐ *Modesty Place* ⌐, which is the **finest** girls' boarding school in the country. I hardly need remind you of the **incident** in the school dining hall yesterday lunchtime. You began by juggling huge bowls of **trifle.** Before long they were z z z o o o m m i n g through the air, heading straight for the teachers' table."

"At least it saved you all the bother of queuing for dessert, Headmistress," replied the little girl. If this was designed to stop Miss Prigg from becoming further enraged, it failed **miserably.**

"I WAS COVERED FROM HEAD TO TOE IN TRIFLE!"
boomed the headmistress, her face now boiling with fury,
her teeth on the verge of gnashing. "Only this morning I
found a piece of *jelly* in my ear."

"Did you eat it, miss?" enquired the girl politely.

"No! I did NOT eat it!"

BOUNCE
SQUEAK!

BOUNCE
SQUEAK!

BOUNCE
SQUEAK!

This noise was really distracting the headmistress now,
but she pressed on. "Then there was the time you caused
chaos in your art class. You jiggled and wiggled and,
before we knew it, there was paint sprayed
across the walls, windows and ceiling..."

"Our art teacher, Miss
Splurge, remarked that
she actually rather liked
the redecoration."

The headmistress
chose to ignore this
smarty-pants reply.

"And the time when you managed to release ALL the lacrosse balls from the games cupboard. Miss Heft, your poor PE teacher, wobbled over and was carried off down the pitch on a sea of them!"

"I do hope they eventually find her," remarked Petula.

"I DO TOO!" bellowed the headmistress.

BOUNCE **BOUNCE** **BOUNCE**
SQUEAK! SQUEAK! SQUEAK!

Miss Prigg couldn't take it a moment longer.

"WILL YOU BE STILL?!" she ordered.

"Sorry, miss," muttered the girl. For a moment Petula was still. But the moment soon passed.

There was a wobble, then a wibble, ending up in a huge wubble. The girl performed a dive roll on to the floor, before finishing her acrobatics display with a handstand.

"Now, *Miss Perpetual-Motion*," purred Miss Prigg with a new hint of menace in her voice, "I need the trip to the **PORCELAIN** museum to pass without incident or Modesty Place – founded one thousand years ago by a nun, no less – could become a laughing stock."

"Of course, miss," said the UPSIDE-DOWN girl who was now scuttling about the headmistress's office on her hands like a performing poodle.

"So I have ordered Modesty Place's science teacher, Professor Blink, to come up with a contraption to stop you causing any damage to the priceless antiques."

Miss Petula Perpetual-Motion did not like the sound of this at all. "I will be fine without it, thank you, miss," she said. The girl's legs were now doing scissor kicks.

As she spoke, her legs sent a pile of school reports
flying off the headmistress's desk.
They looked like a flock of sea gulls taking flight.

"No, you will not!" barked the headmistress.
"What is this contraption, miss?"
"Oh, you'll see!" said Miss Prigg ominously,
desperately trying to pluck the
sheets of paper from the air.

"NOW GET OUT!"

booting the newly out of the study, polished trophies to the floor as she went.

With that, Petula cartwheeled

CRASH!

BANG!

WALLOP!

* * *

The day of the school trip arrived, and Professor Blink proudly wheeled her invention out of the science block and into the playground.

"There we are, Headmistress!" said the lady, still sporting her white lab coat and safety goggles. "Just as you asked."

"It's marvellous, Professor!" replied Miss Prigg.

It looked like a giant toy for a hamster.

The science teacher had created a huge, round, see-through inflatable ball, large enough for someone to be placed inside. Of course, that someone was *Miss Petula Perpetual-Motion*.

"I am proud to finally unveil my invention!" announced the professor. "I have named it

the Bouncing BOOM-BOOM Ball.

"It is destined to stop jiggling children all over the world from destroying everything in their paths."

"KEEP IT BRIEF!" ordered the headmistress, who only liked the sound of her own voice.

"Yes, yes, Headmistress," replied the science teacher hurriedly. "It's very simple – the child who cannot stay still is stuffed in here," she began, indicating a small hatch in the ball. "Then, when the child does fidget, the Bouncing BOOM-BOOM Ball will simply bounce off any precious objects nearby, causing zero damage."

At least that was the idea.

"Splendid!" said the headmistress.

"You may go!"

It was a long coach ride to the **PORCELAIN** museum. Despite the driver's protestations, the headmistress insisted that Petula travel in the boot so she couldn't cause any damage on the way.

As soon as they arrived, the headmistress stuffed *Miss Petula Perpetual-Motion* into the Bouncing **BOOM-BOOM** Ball. Then she led her party of schoolgirls inside the museum as Petula bounced along, bringing up the rear. Despite her initial reluctance, once inside the Bouncing **BOOM-BOOM** Ball the girl began to enjoy it. A smile spread across her face.

The museum was a treasure trove of all things **PORCELAIN**.

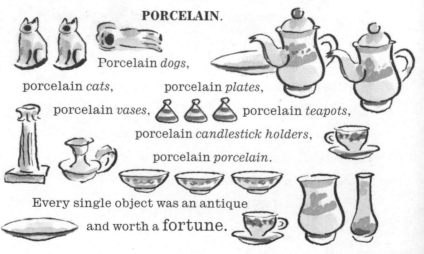

Porcelain *dogs*, porcelain *cats*, porcelain *plates*, porcelain *vases*, porcelain *teapots*, porcelain *candlestick holders*, porcelain *porcelain*.

Every single object was an antique and worth a fortune.

"Now, girls, needless to say, there is absolutely no touching of any of the items on display," announced the headmistress. "I know most of your mamas and papas are filthy rich since they send you to ⟩ *Modesty Place* ⟨, which I am proud to say is the most expensive school in the country. However, if you do touch anything and cause it to break, you will have to pay for it yourselves, every last penny. Does your beloved headmistress make herself clear?"

The pupils murmured.

"I SAID, DOES YOUR BELOVED HEADMISTRESS MAKE HERSELF CLEAR?!"

"Yes, miss," replied the girls.

"Now gather round!"

The girls huddled round a plinth. On it sat a large bowl, with hundreds of tiny flowers hand-painted round the outside. Petula bounced up and down in her giant ball to try to get a better look. Miss Prigg raised her half-moon spectacles to her eyes.

"This bowl was made in Paris. It once belonged to the last queen of France, Marie Antoinette, and dates back to the eighteenth century."

Suddenly, in her eagerness to see, *Miss Petula Perpetual-Motion* bounced so hard that the Bouncing **BOOM-BOOM** Ball hit the ceiling.

From there it rebounded, gathering speed at an

alarming rate. Now it was going

WHAM!

up and down, up and down, up and down, shaking the room as it bounce-bounce-bounced. **BOOM!**

BOOM!

BOOM!

The headmistress gasped in horror. *Miss Petula Perpetual-Motion* was bouncing dangerously close to the priceless **PORCELAIN** pieces.

As the Bouncing **BOOM-BOOM** Ball bounced closer and closer, Miss Prigg stretched out her long thin arms and gave it a shove. This caused the contraption to start ricocheting off the walls. As all the other schoolgirls watched with their mouths open, it walloped off the priceless **PORCELAIN** without damaging it at all, and then bounced back into the headmistress –

BASH!

– sending her tumbling into a **PORCELAIN** penguin posing on a plinth.

"**Noooo!**"

she screamed.

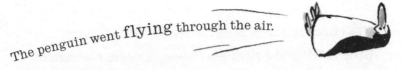

The penguin went flying through the air.

It was an unusual sight as penguins are, of course, flightless birds. But the wonder of seeing such a bird finally taking flight was soon brought to an abrupt halt. The **PORCELAIN** penguin smashed against the wall...

CRASH!

...shattering into hundreds of tiny pieces. All the schoolgirls gasped in horror and **delight**.

"You'll pay for that, *Perpetual-Motion!*" shouted the headmistress.

"But I didn't touch the priceless **PORCELAIN**, Headmistress! You did!" reasoned the girl.

Needless to say, this made Miss Prigg blaze with rage. She chased after *Miss Petula Perpetual-Motion* as the girl bounce-bounce-bounced off to the other side of the room.

BOOM! BOOM! BOOM!

The headmistress raced towards the Bouncing **BOOM-BOOM** Ball, this time with her arms and legs outstretched to stop it. But as it bounced off the wall, it sent the lady flying backwards through the air once more.

The first thing she hit was a **PORCELAIN** statue of a *swan*.

THWACK!

The second thing was a life-sized **PORCELAIN** statue of a *ballerina*.

SMASH!
BANG!

The third thing she hit was a **PORCELAIN** statue of a *clown*.

WALLOP!

It wasn't one of those happy clowns. It was one of those sad clowns. Sadly there isn't time to fully explore the clown's emotional state. That's because said clown, along with those other objects flying through the air, was soon nothing more than a shower of **PORCELAIN** scattering across the floor.

SHATTER!

At this very moment, hearing all the commotion, the elderly museum director came dashing out of his office. He popped his monocle into place to survey the damage. Every single one of the museum's most priceless pieces of **PORCELAIN** was in pieces.

"What is the meaning of this?!"

he bellowed, waving one of his walking sticks aloft in fury.

The headmistress wobbled to her feet, crunching **PORCELAIN** gravel underfoot as she did so.

CRUNCH. CRUNCH. CRUNCH.

"I can explain!" pleaded the lady.

"Who touched the precious, priceless, pleasing **PORCELAIN** pieces?" demanded the museum director.

"Well…" The headmistress glanced over at *Miss Petula Perpetual-Motion* who, to her surprise, was now bouncing only very gently in her plastic ball.

"Well, technically it was ME, but—"

"No buts!" shouted the museum director.

"Lady! **You** will pay for every last piece!"

"NoooooooooooooooooooooooooooooOOOO!!!"

screamed the headmistress.

The girl who couldn't keep **still** smirked.

* * *

The museum's bill came to many millions. On a headmistress's salary, even at the most expensive school in the country, it would have taken a thousand years for Miss Prigg to pay everything back. So she had to take on lots of other jobs at Modesty Place.

Despite being a very grand woman, the headmistress now had to be up at dawn every morning with a mop and bucket, cleaning the school corridors.

At lunchtime she would be dishing out soup in the dining hall.

And after school most days, Miss Prigg could be seen up a ladder, clearing wet leaves and dead pigeons from the guttering.

And if there was one person guaranteed to

KICK over the

headmistress's *bucket,*

send the *soup*

FLYING

through the air,

or **TRIP** over

her *ladder,*

it was of course...

Miss Petula Perpetual-Motion!

* * *

Some years later it was Petula's very last day at
Modesty Place . She was eighteen years old now, and
ready to somersault off into the world.

That morning the headmistress had been up at dawn
unblocking the toilets and she had been called to
the library to clear up some vomit after the librarian had
come down with food poisoning.

As Miss Prigg angrily plonked down her mop
and bucket, she spotted her nemesis,
Petula, sitting in a corner of the library
reading a book.

The strange thing was
that the girl was sitting
perfectly motionless.

Miss Prigg hid behind some shelves of books, and spied
on her most-hated pupil. Apart from turning a page every
couple of minutes, *Miss Petula Perpetual-Motion* did not move
a muscle.

After an hour of snooping the headmistress leaped
out from behind the shelves.

"AHA!" exclaimed the lady. "GOTCHA!"

"Shush!" shushed Petula, her eyes indicating a sign on the wall of the library that said **SILENCE!**

"But, but, but...!" The headmistress couldn't contain herself. "You can sit still if you want to!"

"Yes, I can!" replied the girl. "And I have ALWAYS been able to!"

"But what about that **letter** from your mother?"

"Oh, that silly old thing? I wrote that myself!"

"ONE HUNDRED

YEARS

OF

DETENTION!"

bellowed

Miss Prigg.

"I'd love to, I really would, but today is my very last day at *Modesty Place*. And for old times' sake I am going to...

...**cartwheel** out.
Farewell, Headmistress!"

With that *Miss Petula Perpetual-Motion* leaped on to her hands and spun out of the library, sending every single book flying through the air.

THUD!
THUD!
THUD!

The headmistress was in the library until midnight, picking up all the books and putting them back on the shelves. Then she still had to mop up the vomit.

So now you know, *Miss Petula Perpetual-Motion* really was one of the world's worst children.

WONDERFULLY so.

THESE
CHILDREN GET
WORSER AND
WORSERER!

PETER
Picker

SOME CHILDREN LIKE to blow their nose; some like to pick. Peter was a **picker**. The boy always had a finger up his nose. Sometimes two. One in each nostril.

The buried treasure he was searching for was of purest green:

PETER PICKER

Although he was short for his age, **Peter Picker** could pick an extensive and seemingly endless supply of it.

Runny snot. Gloopy snot. Hard snot. Snot balls. Snot icicles. Snot stalactites. Snot stalagmites.

He was the lord of all that was green and slimy.

After picking, the boy would give his latest morsel of snot a quick inspection, and then add it to his **BALL** of **BOGEYS**.

He had read in a book of world records that the biggest ever bogey recorded was produced by an unsmiling German girl named *Fräulein Schleim*. Hers was the size of a **cannonball**, and weighed as much as a medium-sized pig.*

*Although only twelve, Fräulein Schleim already had a number of unsavoury world records to her name. The girl had produced the world's biggest block of EARWAX, which was the size of a tub of ice cream. Next she was responsible for the world's largest shower of DANDRUFF, managing to completely cover a football pitch just by untying her pigtails. The world record Fräulein Schleim was proudest of, however, was the one for the smelliest FOOT CHEESE. When she took off her steel-toe-capped boots, the stench flattened every tree within a ten-mile radius.

Propelled by the idea that he too could earn a place in *The Book of World Records*, **Peter Picker** set about attempting to smash his rival's effort. He was determined to produce the bogey to end all bogeys — a **GARGANTUAN** ball of snot.

He had started with just one ordinary, medium-sized bogey. However, once he had stuck bogey after bogey to it, it became a super-bogey. Then a **MEGA-BOGEY**. Finally it progressed to being an **ULTRA-BOGEY**.

Now, every time the boy picked his nose (which was at least once every few seconds), he added to it. When Peter started, it was just the size of a pea. But with each new green globule it grew. Soon it was the size of a conker, then a melon, then a football, then a snowman.

The boy became so focused on entering the record books that he often bunked off school so he could spend all day picking his nose.

PETER PICKER

At first Peter was able to carry this ball of snot around
with him. When it became too big and heavy, the boy
simply rolled it along the street.

However, one morning on the way to school, Peter had
accidentally run over his neighbour's cat, Ginger,
and the poor creature had become embedded
in the snot ball.

"MEOW!!!"

The bogey was so sticky Peter had to
shave the cat's hair off to remove it.

"MMMEEEOOOWWW!!!"

Now the boy kept the sphere of snot safe in
his bedroom. By the time of this story, the
sphere of snot (or SNOT-SPHERE for short)
was the size of an asteroid. It looked like
it had come from outer space too.

A kaleidoscope of greens.
Light green.
Dark green.
Green green.
Not-so-green green.

But, with new bogeys being picked, licked and flicked on to it by the minute, Peter's **SNOT-SPHERE** was becoming too big even for his bedroom. The boy's bed and wardrobe were crushed by the size and weight of this truly evil-looking **ULTRA-BOGEY**.

One morning, while rooting around in his nostril, Peter found a particularly large bogey. Without a second thought he wiped it on the **SNOT-SPHERE**, but this was one final piece too many, and the boy heard a buckling sound. **TWANG!**

It was the floorboards creaking under the enormous weight of the **ULTRA-BOGEY**.

Peter raced out of his room and downstairs to the kitchen. Looking up at the ceiling, he saw cracks shooting across it. **CRACK!**

Then, before Peter could pick his nose again, the **SNOT-SPHERE** crashed down through the ceiling and landed next to him. **BOOM!**

"Argh!" screamed the boy as dust and debris covered him. Peter had very nearly been killed by his own mucus.

And it was on a roll now, literally, and heading straight for the boy. Peter dashed out of his house, but the

SNOT-SPHERE smashed through the front wall...

CRASH!

...and chased its creator down the street.

Peter's parents stared down from their bedroom window. Their mouths were wide open, but no sound came out, such was their shock at the scene.

Being made of compacted bogeys, the **SNOT~SPHERE** was incredibly **STICKY**. As a result, it picked up everything in its path as it rolled:

a little **dog**,

an **old lady** who was walking said little dog,

a **bicycle**,

a **boy** riding said bicycle,

a **lawnmower**,

a **gardener** using said lawnmower.

Soon all these things and more were spinning wildly down the road, stuck to the **SNOT~SPHERE**.

Peter's bogey was growing bigger and bigger. The bigger the bogey became, the faster it ROLLED.

As Peter kept running and running and running away from it, the **SNOT-SPHERE** picked up a **postbox** and uprooted a **tree**. Even a **car** became stuck to it.

When the ever-growing **SNOT-SPHERE** rolled on top of a bus full of people and managed to glue itself to the roof, Peter really began to panic.

As the people on the bus spun round and round, like visitors to some nightmarish, snot-themed **AMUSEMENT PARK**, the boy realised he was running for his life.

Now the **SNOT-SPHERE** was so huge it was picking up houses as it rolled. First a bungalow, then a large family home.

What with the **house**, the
bungalow, the **bus**, the **car**, the **tree**, the **postbox**, the **lawnmower**, the **gardener** using the lawnmower, the **bicycle**, the **boy** riding the bicycle, the little **dog** and, of course, let's not forget the **old lady** who was out walking her little dog, all stuck to it, the **SNOT-SPHERE** was growing at a truly alarming rate.

Peter had a plan. The only way he could survive was to go **underground.** That's where the **SNOT-SPHERE** could not reach him. Up ahead the boy spied a drain and dashed towards it. Desperately, he pulled on the grate with all his strength.

"Please, please, please!" he incanted.

His fingers slipped on the metal. They were wet and **withered** from being up his nose all day.

Just in time Peter managed to pull the grate off and leap down into the murky depths below.

SPLASH!

The **SNOT-SPHERE** rumbled overhead.

RUMBLE!

Peter breathed a huge sigh of relief, which echoed around the drain.

"AH!"

AH! AH! AH! AH! AH! AH! AH!

When he felt it was safe again, the boy climbed back up to the surface, covered in grot from the drain. Peter watched as the giant **SNOT-SPHERE** spun off into the distance, picking up everything in its path.

A **fire engine**,
a **parade of shops**,
even a **herd of cows**
who had been minding
their own business,
getting on with
some quiet
MOOING.

"MOO!"
"MOO!"
"MOO!"

Seeing the mass destruction his creation had caused, **Peter Picker** decided it was probably best not to mention to anyone that he was the creator of this snot-based ball of **TERROR**. With all that had happened, he was willing to let *Fräulein Schleim* retain the title for the world's biggest bogey.

So Peter ambled down the road towards school. It was the first time he had attended for weeks. However, when Peter arrived at the school gates, he realised his school was, in fact, no longer there.

There were just dark patches on the playground where the school buildings used to be.

Peter's spinning ball of **DOOM** must have rolled ahead of him this way too and sucked all the school buildings up into it.

All that could be seen was a lone pair of Wellington boots, standing where the dining hall used to be. The boots had belonged to the fearsome dinner lady, Mrs Slaughter. No doubt she and all the teachers had been plucked up by the **MEGA-BOGEY** too.

Peter smirked. **"Ha ha!**

At least now I don't have to go to school ever again!" he chuckled, as he stood alone in the playground, feeling like the last man on Earth.

Then, just as he was about to turn round and head home (or at least to what was left of his home), Peter heard a sound behind him...

It was getting

louder and louder

by the moment.

A rumbling

sound,

a thundering

sound,

a DEAFENING

sound.

The ground was shaking

beneath the boy's feet.

Peter gulped in fear.

GULP!

He knew full well what it was.
He could barely bring himself to turn
round to face it. But he had to. Slowly
he twisted his neck, and saw that the great
SNOT-SPHERE must have rolled all the way round
the Earth and was now heading back – straight for him!

By now it was the size of a moon, and had picked up various landmarks on its epic journey. The **Eiffel Tower**, the **Roman Colosseum**, an **Egyptian pyramid**, and the **Houses of Parliament** – all were sticking out of it like Flakes in a Mr Whippy ice cream.

Buckingham Palace had been pulled out of the ground and rolled away too, exposing *Her Majesty the Queen*, red-faced and sitting on the loo.

"AAARRRGGGHHH!!!"

Peter screamed as the thing sped closer and closer.

The **MEGA-BOGEY** was by now so **MEGATASTICAL** that it blocked out the sun. A HUGE dark shadow fell across the boy and he felt cold.

Peter closed his eyes in terror as the **SNOT-SPHERE** rolled over him and plucked him clean off the ground.

"NOOOOO!!!"

The top of the boy's head was instantly embedded in the ball as it thundered its way off back round the Earth.

But *Her Majesty the Queen* was angry that everyone had seen her on the loo so she ordered her palace guards to fire their cannon at the **SNOT-SPHERE**.

"Fire at will!"

The **cannonball** zoooooomed towards the giant bogey.

КАВ

OOM!

The **SNOT-SPHERE**

exploded

into pieces

that began

to fall back

down to earth,

returning everyone and
everything to their rightful places.

Except one boy.

Peter was still stuck in a huge chunk of snot.
This piece flew through the air, only to land
on top of **St Paul's Cathedral**.

His parents visited every Sunday and hurled him titbits from the ground. **Peter Picker** remained stuck to the spire for the rest of his life, upside down in his own GIANT bogey.

Which is, of course, what can happen if YOU pick your nose. Next time, have a **blow**.

Grubby
GERTRUDE

Do you know an extremely **dirty** child? A grimy girl? A foul-smelling boy? However dirty and stinky they might be, they could never compare to Grubby Gertrude. This was a girl who delighted in being the dirtiest child in the world! Soap and water were complete strangers to Gertrude. Everywhere she went, a huge cloud of dust and dirt and pong followed her.

Needless to say, everything Grubby Gertrude touched became grubby too. Her schoolbooks were splattered and stained with *unspeakable* things. And, despite her mother's protestations, Gertrude refused to let her clothes be washed, so in no time they became encrusted with dirt too.

However, the grubbiest thing in Gertrude's life was her bedroom. Although her mother begged her to tidy it, Gertrude never, ever did.

She simply dropped

everything on the floor.

It was as if her room

was her own personal

rubbish dump.

Over time the pile of **pongy trainers,**
snotty tissues,   **half-eaten egg sandwiches**
and **hamster droppings**   that had
gone white and crumbly* came up to Gertrude's knees.

The only way Gertrude could make it to her mucky
bed was to wade through tons of rubbish. The bedroom
carpet was a distant memory: it had not been seen for
years. But, being one of the world's WORST children,
Gertrude loved living knee-deep in filth. The grubbier
the better.

Now let me take a moment to tell you about Gertrude's
feet. They were so grubby they looked like those of
a troll.

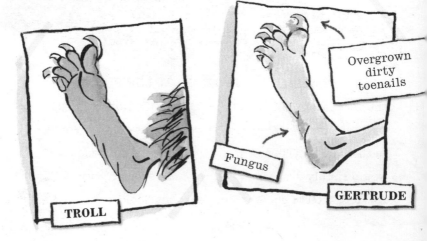

Overgrown
dirty
toenails

Fungus

GERTRUDE

TROLL

* Doo-Doo the hamster had long since disappeared.

Each foot was covered in a green fungus, and she had long *curling* toenails that she refused to cut. As a result, her feet smelled even worse than runny cheese that had gone off decades ago. When Gertrude peeled each sock off at the end of the day, she would lift it to her nose.

"Mmmmmmmmmmm!" the girl would sigh in pleasure.

You or I would have screamed at the smell or, at the very least, projectile-vomited. Not Gertrude. She was over the moon that her socks were the pongiest in the world. Then, like everything else, Gertrude would simply drop them on top of the ever-growing mountain of *muck* on her bedroom floor.

"Please tidy your room this instant!" Gertrude's mother would plead. The poor lady was in torment.

She prided herself on keeping the rest of her house utterly spotless. If a single biscuit crumb dropped on to the carpet, Mother would get the vacuum cleaner out. The grubbiness of Gertrude's bedroom was absolutely horrifying to her. How had she, a lady who always kept a vase of fresh flowers on the dining table, given birth to a child who chose to live in a... swamp?

"BOG OFF!" Gertrude would reply with a laugh. She knew that her mother (always immaculately turned out with her hair in a swirl and a string of pearls round her neck) loathed her saying the word 'BOG'. So Gertrude always, always, always made sure she used it when speaking to her.

"Daughter! I forbid you from using that foul word!" Mother would wail.

"What? 'BOG'?" Gertrude would answer mischievously.

"Yes. It's a *frightful* word that has no place in my otherwise delightful home. Now, young lady, I need you to tidy your room this instant!"

"BOG OFF!" Gertrude would shout back.

If the girl **wouldn't** tidy her room then her mother decided that *she* would. As soon as Gertrude left for school one morning, Mother put her plan into action. Armed with **thick** rubber gloves and a roll of a hundred pink perfumed bin bags, she hurtled upstairs with her sleeve over her nose and mouth (such was the **STINKORAMA**).

"CHARGE!"

she bellowed as if going into battle.

With all her might Mother **hurled** herself against her daughter's bedroom door.

"HUMPH!"

But the door would only open a tiny bit. The pile of *grot* had grown to **waist height.**

"ARGH!" screamed Mother as she sneaked a peek through the crack in the door at the sea of filth.

"URGH!" she bellowed as the pong hit her smack on the nose.

The problem was that, try as she might, Gertrude's mother couldn't get inside her daughter's room. Gertrude could just about squeeze her little body through and surf over the rubbish. For her mother that was impossible.

The lady was about to admit defeat when...

PING!

...she had an idea.

Keeping the door wedged open with her shoe, she hopped back down the stairs to grab her vacuum cleaner. She pushed the long hose of the machine through the gap in Gertrude's door, and flicked the switch.

BUZZ!

The lady was delighted as the nozzle started sucking things up...

A full carton of chocolate milkshake that had turned rancid.

A pus-filled plaster.

A lump of mouldy cheese.

Mother smiled to herself. By the time her daughter was back from school, she might just have the rubbish down to ankle height.

At that moment the vacuum cleaner made an awful droning noise... **uGuGuGuGuG!**

...before there was a sound of metal being crunched. **CRUNK!**

The vacuum cleaner shook violently and exploded.

BANG!

Mother was covered from head to toe in all the things the machine had sucked up.

"The horror! The horror!" she wailed at being caked in **dirt**, **dust** and rancid **chocolate milkshake**, among other things.

She bent down to examine her vacuum cleaner.
It had been smashed to pieces.

Something
EXTREMELY big
and strong must
have broken it.

Was there *something* lurking under the rubbish in her
daughter's bedroom that could have done that?

"Hell-o?" called Mother.

There was no answer.

The lady dismissed it as a foolish thought. The
vacuum cleaner must have somehow destroyed itself. She
staggered to the bathroom, desperate to get clean.
When Gertrude returned from school her mother was

still in the bath, her twenty-seventh that day. Before the lady could say anything, the girl had dashed up the stairs and squeezed herself back into her bedroom.

Using an old plastic tray from a fast-food restaurant, Gertrude surfed across the rubbish to her bed. There she peeled off her damp socks. A pair that had been worn hundreds of times without ever being washed. Gertrude was delighted to see that fungus had begun to appear on them.

Rummaging deep down in the murky depths of her muck, the girl found another sock that she had dropped there many years before.

This one had a number of unusual-looking growths sprouting out of it – like misshapen vegetables from distant solar systems. Gertrude realised her grubbiness had reached such an epic level that things were growing out of it.

However, nothing could prepare the girl for what was about to happen...

Lying in her filthy bed that night, between sheets that were *slimy* with grime, Gertrude noticed something MOVING AROUND in the mucky darkness.

Surely the girl's mind was playing tricks on her.

Was she *dreaming?*

"BOG OFF!" she called out, just in case there really was *something* hiding down there.

Whatever it was moved again.

The smaller bits of rubbish on the grot-surface rustled as something swam underneath.

GRUBBY GERTRUDE

This was **no** dream. Or even nightmare. This was **really** happening. There was something living **UNDER** the rubbish in Grubby Gertrude's bedroom.

Could it be a *rat*?

No, this thing seemed too **big** to be a rat.

A giant *cockroach* perhaps?

No, it didn't S C U T T L E like a *cockroach*.

Surely not a *deadly snake*?

No, this thing didn't **hiss**...

It growled.

"GRRRRRRR!"

There was only one explanation.

This was some other kind of... **creature.**

A creature that had hatched out of the *murky* depths of the girl's muck.

A creature previously unknown to humankind.

In a desperate attempt to keep the thing at bay, Gertrude bounced on her bed until she reached high enough to leap up on to the top of her wardrobe. There she had stockpiled some grot for a special occasion. No matter, she needed it this instant.

GRUBBY GERTRUDE

With all her **might** she threw down

some half-empty **yogurt pots**,

a stash of pepperoni **pizza crusts**

and a bag of
elephant dung that
she had collected on
a school visit to the zoo.

Next, Gertrude threw herself off the wardrobe
to land heavily on top of her new pile of rubbish,
trying to squash the thing *underneath*.

Little did the girl know that all she was really
doing was feeding the creature.

After stamping about for a while, Gertrude had a lie-down on her bed once more. Exhausted, she closed her eyes.

But, in that place between awake and asleep, Gertrude heard the growling noise again.

"GRRRRRR!"

The girl sat bolt upright in her bed and shouted, "BOG OFF! Whatever is under there, can you just

BOG RIGHT OFF?!"

Her mother must have heard this as she rushed out of the bathroom, her frilly pink dressing gown wafting as she ran.

"GERTRUDE? Is everything all right in there, dear?!" she called from the other side of the door.

"Yeah. Just BOG OFF!"

"No, I will not, you *foul*-mouthed child! Now tell me, who were you talking to?" demanded Mother.

"YOU! NOW BOG RIGHT OFF!!!"

Once again the lady tried to push against the bedroom door. But the mountain of grot was even higher than before and now it was impossible to open the door AT ALL.

"I want you to tidy your room first thing in the morning!" declared Mother. Then she rushed back to the bathroom to try and scrub the last of the rancid chocolate milkshake off her body.

In Gertrude's bedroom, there was a distinctive sound of munching.

MUNCH! MUNCH! MUNCH!

It sounded as if the creature was devouring everything in sight.

"BUUUURRRPPP!!!"

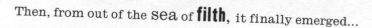

Then, from out of the sea of filth, it finally emerged...

THE **RUBBISH** MONSTER.

It wasn't that it was a
rubbish monster –
it was actually terrifying.
It was called a Rubbish
Monster because it was
made of rubbish.

GRUBBY GERTRUDE

Every part of it was made from something the girl had
deposited on her bedroom floor.

Two ears sat atop the monster's head that had

once been a pair of Gertrude's **pongy socks**.

Its eyes were a couple of slices of pepperoni from an old, **furry pizza**.

The monster's mouth was a **mould-encrusted burger**.

Its bulging body was made up of everything

from **soggy PE kit** and **snotty tissues**

to **sweaty Wellington boots**

and **half-sucked sweets** covered in **dog hair**.

All bound together by **manky plasters**.

It was a truly **MONSTROUS** sight. Which is
what you would expect from a monster.

"BOG OFF!" shouted Gertrude.

She couldn't believe her eyes.
Somehow her rubbish had *fused* together
to create a **mutant** being.

Pacing the girl's bedroom, the monster
began scooping up the rest of the mess
that Gertrude had dropped on the floor.

It was quick work as the monster's hands were enormous. Each scoop was then stuffed into its mouth.

Old damp **magazines**, dog-chewed **slippers**, withered **balloons**, a long-forgotten **dolly** and **dirty socks**. Mouthfuls and mouthfuls of **dirty** socks.

The monster loved Gertrude's dirty socks. As it ate and ate and ate, it grew at an incredible rate. In no time at all, the monster was so big its head hit the ceiling. **BOINK!**

"Carry on eating, Monster!" ordered Gertrude, a smug smile spreading across her grubby face, because she had realised something...

Her mother had told her to tidy her room thousands of times.

Now a monster was doing it FOR her!

In no time at all, the room was perfectly clean and tidy. Finally you could see the carpet again. And now that the monster had cleared her bedroom Gertrude could start filling it with rubbish *all over again*.

"Thank you SO much," she said. "You may kindly BOG OFF now."

But the monster didn't go. Oh no. It still looked **HUNGRY.** It turned to face the girl. Its gruesome **pepperoni** eyes focused directly on Gertrude.

"*Noooooo!*" she pleaded as it advanced towards her.

That the monster moved so slowly made it all the more terrifying.

PLOD. PLOD. PLOD.

"BOG OFF!" she shouted.

It was too late. The monster picked Gertrude up and *swallowed* her in one **GULP.**

"BUUUUUUUUUUURRRRRRRRRRP!!!!!!!!"

burped the monster.
Grubby Gertrude had paid
the **ultimate** price for her
grubbiness. A monster made
from the girl's own muck
had devoured her.
So, next time a
grown-up tells you to
TIDY YOUR
ROOM, just
DO IT.
Or this may happen to
you…

MY EYES
ARE WATERING
AT THE
SMELL!

CHARLIE
the Chucker

WORLD'S WORST CHILDREN don't come any
naughtier than Charlie Cheung. Charlie was a little boy
who loved chucking snowballs. He was delighted
when the freezing-cold winter arrived, and the first
flakes of snow fell from the sky. Then he would race
outside to catch the tiny white flecks in his hand before

squishing, squashing and squooshing them together to make a big ball of snow.

A snowball!

Next, Charlie would look down into his palm with glee. It was time to make mischief!

"HUH! HUH! HUH!" he would snigger.

Now, I must tell you, and this is important, Charlie was NOT one of those children who loved snowball fights. In a snowball fight, there was far too great a risk of him being hit by a snowball. That was something Charlie hated. Shards of ice snaking down the back of his neck made him howl...

"BOO-HOO-HOO!"

...even though it was exactly what Charlie loved doing to others. This boy needed his snowball fights to be completely one-sided. He had to chuck all the snowballs! Not just that, Charlie loved to plan SURPRISE attacks. He would hide behind a wall, or up a tree, or under a bench.

Then he would wait until his victim was near and
CHUCK!

Charlie would chuck his snowballs at anyone and
anything!

His little sister, Gemma...

DONK! "OUCH!"

"HUH! HUH! HUH!"

An old lady out walking her dog...

DONK!

"OOOH!" "WOOF!"

"HUH! HUH! HUH!"

A squirrel perched on the branch of a tree...

DONK!

"EEK!"

"HUH! HUH! HUH!"

His piano teacher passing by on her bicycle...

DONK! "OOF!"

"HUH! HUH! HUH!"

His little sister, Gemma, again...!

- DONK!

"STOP! It's not funny!"

"It's funny for me!

HUH! HUH! HUH!"

The postman...

DONK! "OUCH!"

"HUH! HUH! HUH!"

Next-door's cat...

DONK!

"MIAOW!"

"HUH! HUH! HUH!"

One of Gemma's precious dolls...

DONK! TOPPLE!

"HUH! HUH! HUH!"

A bird flying high in the sky...

DONK! "SQUAWK!"

"HUH! HUH! HUH!"

Even a poor postbox that was standing
perfectly still minding its own business...!

DONK! THUNK!

"HUH! HUH! HUH!"

Of course, Charlie just had to hit his poor little sister
with a snowball one more time!

DONK!

"OUCH! That was my bottom!"

"HUH! HUH! HUH!"

"How would you like it if I chucked a snowball at your bottom?"

"You never will!"

"I will get you back!"

"Until then, have another one!

DONK!

HUH! HUH! HUH!"

Like many naughty children, Charlie wanted MORE, MORE, MORE! For him that meant MORE, MORE, MORE **MAYHEM!**

It was all well and good lobbing one snowball at a time, but this wasn't enough for little Charlie. How could he throw two snowballs at once?

Charlie was right-handed, but he practised throwing with his left hand too. Soon he could chuck a snowball from each hand at the same time!

This meant **DOUBLE TROUBLE!**

He could hit two targets at once!

Gemma and her favourite doll.

DONK!

DONK!

"ARGH!"

TOPPLE!

"HUH! HUH! HUH!"

However, two snowballs at a time still wasn't enough for Charlie. So he did something rather unusual: he practised gripping snowballs with his feet. Yes, his feet!

Soon, he'd learned to lie on his back and chuck with both his feet and both his hands

AT THE SAME TIME!

This our Charlie did one afternoon in the garden of his family home. He lay in wait in the snow for his sister and her three best friends to come home from school.

This would be a new first for Charlie!

QUADRUPLE TROUBLE!

The boy lay on the ground, hiding behind a bush. When he spied the girls entering through the garden gate, he chucked all four snowballs at once!

DONK! DONK! DONK! DONK!

"URGH!" "ARGH!" "OOCH!" "YIKES!"

The three girls had come over for tea after school to play with Gemma's huge collection of dolls. Now they fled in fear!

"ARGH!"

As Gemma stamped her foot in fury at her naughty brother...

S T A M P !

...Charlie did what he always did. He smirked and sniggered!

"HUH! HUH! HUH!"

Even though chucking four snowballs all at once was quite an achievement, it wasn't enough for him. He wanted to throw more snowballs at a time than anyone had ever done in the history of snowball-throwing. The boy decided he wanted to achieve the impossible...

He would throw one hundred snowballs all at once! And his target would be **every** single person at his school!

Charlie hated going to school after getting in trouble time and time again for throwing snowballs at everyone, including the teachers. Yes, he really was that naughty. Now he wanted to splat a snowball in the face of the headteacher, all the other teachers AND each and every pupil, all at once!

Like all humans, Charlie didn't have enough hands or feet to throw one hundred snowballs at the same time. (Unless you might be reading this book with fifty pairs of hands, then please forgive me.)

So Charlie soon realised he had to invent something to make his dream come true. He began thinking up a contraption to become the greatest snowball-thrower in the history of the world.

The day our story begins, Charlie began sketching what such a device could look like.

He stayed up all through the night and by morning he'd created his masterpiece. Charlie called it the...

SUPERCHUCKER!

The **SUPERCHUCKER** looked a little like a medieval catapult.

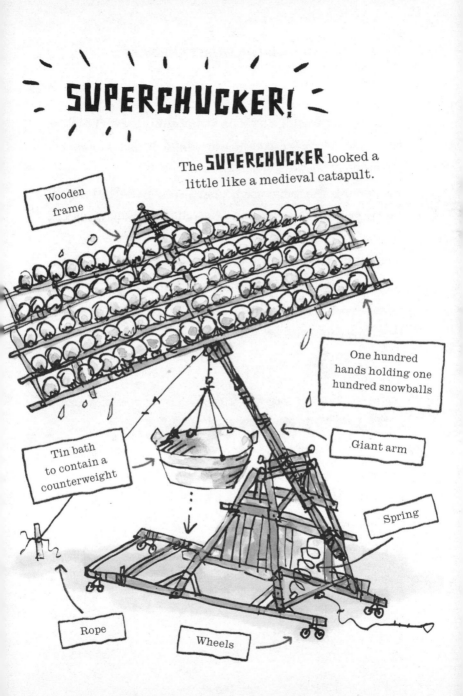

Wooden frame

One hundred hands holding one hundred snowballs

Tin bath to contain a counterweight

Giant arm

Spring

Rope

Wheels

The theory was that as soon as the counterweight in the tin bucket was released, every one of these hundred hands would chuck a snowball.

Now came the tricky part. Charlie had to build this beast. But where would a ten-year-old boy find all the stuff he needed?

First, he "borrowed" all the wood for the contraption's frame from his father's garden shed. Charlie was one hundred per cent sure his father would say no if he asked him if he could destroy his shed and use the timber. So he just didn't ask him. Perfect. Instead, Charlie chopped up the shed.

CHOP! CHOP! CHOP!

Next, he fixed the planks of wood together to build the frame for his **SUPERCHUCKER.**

Then, he "borrowed" the wheels of his little sister's roller skates and fixed them to the bottom of the contraption. Once again, it was better not to ask! So, he didn't. It made life so much simpler.

Next, Charlie needed some rope. So, he "borrowed"

his mother's washing line, with all his father's undercrackers still attached.

After that, Charlie spotted his little sister's toy **Slinky**. This would be the perfect spring he needed for his **SUPERCHUCKER!** Gemma was about to let it down from the top of the stairs when her big brother appeared at the bottom.

"I just need your **Slinky!**" he announced as he bounded up the stairs and grabbed the end of it.

"GET OFF!" yelled Gemma.

"JUST LET GO!" shouted Charlie, bounding back down the stairs with one end of the **Slinky**.

"IT'S MY **SLINKY!**" she cried.

"Give this **Slinky** to me!"

"Or what?"

"Or I will yank it out of your hands!" he stated.

"You will have to yank it because I am **not** letting go!" she fibbed. Gemma had every intention of letting go. She just had to pick the right moment when the **Slinky** was fully stretched... Then it would cause the mightiest STING!

"I WILL PULL THAT SLINKY OUT OF YOUR HANDS!" yelled Charlie.

"GO ON, THEN!"

"THREE! TWO! ONE! HUH!"

As soon as Charlie yanked hard, Gemma let go.

The SLINKY shot back.

TWANG!

It whacked Charlie bang on the nose!

BOFF!

"Aaahhh! What did you do that for?" moaned Charlie.

"I thought you wanted my **Slinky?**"

"I did, but... Never mind!"

"Tee! Hee! Hee!" chuckled Gemma.

"Huh! Huh! Huh!" sniggered Charlie to himself. Only *he* knew what MONKEY BUSINESS he was up to.

Now there was just one final part needed to make the **SUPERCHUCKER.**

The hundred hands.

But where on earth would he find them? Charlie only had two and he was rather attached to them.

This seemed like the hardest part of all.

Then Charlie had a thought.

A **dark** thought.

A **wicked** thought.

A thought so **BAD** it makes Charlie one of the world's worst children of all time!

His little sister's doll collection!

Gemma was the proud owner of fifty pretty dolls. She kept them in pride of place on shelves in her bedroom.

So, while Gemma was sleeping soundly that night, Charlie tiptoed into her bedroom.

One by one, he snatched all his sister's dolls before piling them up in his own room. Once safely inside, Charlie locked the door and took out a sharp pair of scissors.

Now, this is not for the faint-hearted, but Charlie did something so horrid I almost dare not tell you. (Almost.)

Yes, you guessed it.

Charlie snipped off the hands of all fifty dolls!

SNIP! SNIP! SNIP!

Soon the wicked boy had one hundred little plastic hands!

Next, he rushed outside into the snow with his haul. It was time to attach all the hands to his

SUPERCHUCKER!

Once he had done that, Charlie stepped back to admire his genius creation. Looking at it, he realised he'd forgotten one last, rather important thing.

"The counterweight!" he exclaimed.

Charlie needed to put this in place before loading the SUPERCHUCKER with snowballs. Once the counterweight was removed, it would release the spring and chuck all the snowballs!

Charlie scurried around the garden, looking for something that was just heavy enough to work.

A flowerpot?
No.

A dustbin?
No.

A birdbath?
No.

Charlie glanced up at his sister's window. The boy was sure he'd seen a curtain twitch, but it was still. Maybe he had imagined it.

Then a thought struck him like a lightning bolt!

ZAP!

YES! Gemma herself would be the perfect counterweight!

So Charlie tiptoed upstairs and slowly opened her bedroom door.

The girl was now snoring loudly.

"ZZZ! ZZZZ! ZZZZZ!"

Charlie thought this was a little strange, as he had never heard his sister snore before. No matter. He

hoisted Gemma over his shoulder and carried her
down the stairs. Then he placed her in the tin bath.

TWUNK!

Now that he had the perfect counterweight,
Charlie was ready to ROLL!

"Thank goodness she hasn't woken up!"
he hissed to himself, absolutely amazed.

Gemma carried on snoring loudly,
standing upright in the bath. **"ZZZZZ!**
ZZZZZZ!"

Charlie scooped up handfuls of fresh powdery snow
from all over the garden.

Then he loaded each plastic hand with a snowball.

Soon he had his haul of one hundred snowballs! Next,
Charlie wheeled his **SUPERCHUCKER** all the way to
school, making sure he arrived super early.

Once Charlie had passed through the school gates, he crossed the empty playground and hid himself and his evil invention behind the bicycle sheds. Soon the playground began to fill with pupils and teachers arriving for the school day.

Once it was full, Charlie put on a very **deep** grown-up's voice and shouted,

"THIS IS THE SCHOOL INSPECTOR SPEAKING. PLEASE COULD EVERYONE, PUPILS AND TEACHERS, GATHER IN THE CENTRE OF THE PLAYGROUND FOR A SPECIAL ANNOUNCEMENT!"

To Charlie's astonishment, everyone did exactly as they were told. Well, they weren't naughty like him. His fiendish plan was working a treat.

They were all about to get SNOWBALLED!

"HUH! HUH! HUH!"

Craftily, Gemma opened one eye. It was clear by the twinkle in it that she had been awake all this time. The girl was up to something! She was waiting for the perfect moment to strike! As soon as her brother looked in her direction, she shut her eye and went back to snoring.

"**ZZZZZ! ZZZZZZ!"**

Charlie wheeled her and his **SUPERCHUCKER** into the playground.

The one hundred people stood still, open-mouthed in shock. What on earth was this bizarre thing?

Bits of an old shed?

A washing line with undercrackers still on it?

A **Slinky?**

A snoring girl in her pyjamas, standing up in a tin bath?

Roller-skate wheels?

And, weirdest of all, one hundred plastic hands, each holding a snowball?

While they all stood there gawping, Charlie put his **SUPERCHUCKER** in place. All the teachers and pupils were now in range of the snowballs. All he had to do was release the counterweight. Then the giant arm would spring forward and…

DONK! DONK! DONK! A hundred times!

Everyone in the school would be SNOWBALLED.

"HUH! HUH! HUH!"

But Gemma had other ideas. She opened both eyes now and shouted to the crowd: "RUN! RUN! RUN! SNOWBALLS INCOMING!"

Run they did!

"GEMMA! YOU ARE AWAKE!" barked a furious Charlie.

"Aren't you clever…" purred Gemma.

"What are you doing?" he demanded.

"I'm getting my own back for what you did to my beautiful dolls."

"B-b-but—!"

"No buts, Charlie. Now it's time for a taste of your own medicine!" she said.

Charlie tried to run away, but, without thinking, he ran straight into the line of fire.

Gemma leaped off the **SUPERCHUCKER.**

TWONG!

The *Slinky* sprang shut and the one hundred snowballs were launched into the air.

WHOOSH!

Charlie looked back aghast as one hundred snowballs sped towards him.

WHIZZ!

The snowballs hit him all at once!

DONK! DONK! DONK!

"ARGH!" he cried.

Not that anyone could hear him, as he was now trapped inside a giant snowball!

"HA! HA! HA!" laughed everyone, no one harder than Gemma.

Charlie was **fuming**. He hated being hit by snowballs,

and now he was trapped inside one. He was frozen in a giant ball of snow. The boy tried and tried and tried to wriggle free, but all he did was cause the giant snowball to roll...

TRUNDLE!

As it did so, it picked up all the snow on the playground.

It got BIGGER

and BIGGER

and BIGGER.

TRUNDLE!

Now, Gemma may have found her big brother extremely annoying, but she didn't want him to be trapped inside a giant snowball forever.

"LET'S GET HIM OUT!" she cried.

So the mass of people in the playground chased after the snowball.

They ran ahead of it and pushed it back, but, instead of stopping, the giant snowball rolled and rolled and rolled in the opposite direction.

TRUNDLE!

As it did so, it picked up more and more and more snow, getting BIGGER and BIGGER and BIGGER!

It was now larger than a hot-air balloon. Charlie's worst nightmare had come true! To make matters worse, the giant snowball was now heading straight for the

SUPERCHUCKER!

TRUNDLE!

Gemma leaped out of the way.

WHOOMPH!

The giant snowball smashed straight into the
SUPERCHUCKER!

KERUNCH!

Both broke into hundreds of pieces!

SMASH!

Charlie landed on the playground.

BOOF!

CHARLIE THE CHUCKER

He was frozen solid like a giant ice lolly.

At last, Charlie the Chucker had got his comeuppance!

"HA! HA! HA!" laughed everyone at the school.

Charlie was placed by the radiator, and he took until the end of the school day to thaw out.

Now, Gemma was not going to let her brother forget this in a hurry, of course. To make amends, she forced him to...

Rebuild the shed...

Hang up the washing line...

Wash and iron all their father's undercrackers...

Repair her roller skates...

Buy her a brand-new **Slinky**...

And, most importantly, glue each and every hand back on her collection of dolls.

After that, Gemma made Charlie make a solemn promise.

"I promise never, ever to throw a snowball again!" he announced.

"Thank you, Charlie," replied Gemma.

"Now, if you will excuse me, I must just pop out to the shops to buy a massive bag of **WATER BALLOONS!**"

"NOOOOOOOOOOO!" she cried.

"HUH! HUH! HUH!" he sniggered.

Well, what did you expect? Charlie wasn't one of the world's worst children for nothing!

BOINK!

SPLOOSH!

NO MORE
SNOWBALLS!

Windy
MINDY

ONCE UPON A TIME there was a little girl who was known as **Windy Mindy**.

Way back when she was a baby, Mindy discovered she had the most awful talent for breaking **wind**. Bubble bombs, thurps, **TOILET TUNES**, putt-putts, UNDER-BURPS, trouser toots, **BLURTS**, bench-warmers, LITTLE TOMMY SQUEAKERS, HONKERS, **bottom yodels**, call them what you will, Mindy would delight in letting them rip.

WINDY MINDY

The little girl was so good at trumping, she could compete in it for her country.*

Mindy's wind took on many different shapes and sizes. The little girl could do SILENT ones, **LOUD** ones, **DEAFENING** ones, l o n g ones, SHORT ones, ones that went **rat-tat-tat** like a machine gun and even explosive ones.

Mindy's was a talent that appalled everyone unfortunate enough to be near her. But the little girl was full of mischief and absolutely loved the chaos her wind caused. There would be STAMPEDES in supermarkets, CHARGES in churches and PANDEMONIUM in patisseries. People would often be trampled underfoot as they tried to escape the smell.

*If there was an international competition that awarded medals for particularly loud or smelly trumps which, at the time of this book going to print, there sadly is not.

Mindy would **deliberately** fill herself up with food she knew would make her bottom burp. She would devour all of the following in gigantic quantities:

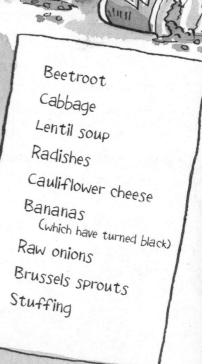

Baked beans
Prune juice
Dried figs
Porridge
Brown sauce
Sherbert
Turnips
Mushy peas
Sweetcorn
Curried eggs
Fizzy pop

Beetroot
Cabbage
Lentil soup
Radishes
Cauliflower cheese
Bananas
(which have turned black)
Raw onions
Brussels sprouts
Stuffing

At school the teachers would often send Mindy out of lessons for her *'outbursts'*. Mindy would claim it was an accident, but the truth was she did it on purpose.

Every single time.

Either the noise would be so disruptive, or the smell so overpowering, that the classroom had to be evacuated. Then off Mindy would be sent to the headmistress's office, where she would be given a stern ticking-off.

"Mindy, I am extremely disappointed in you," announced the headmistress on the particular morning that our story begins. The lady kept the door of her office open as a precaution, just in case the little girl let another one go.

"Sorry, Headmistress," said Mindy with a smirk.

"This is the *twelfth* time this week a teacher has sent you to my office. And it's only Tuesday."

"I said sorry!"

"Sorry isn't good enough! Today Miss Prism had to send you out of her maths lesson for making '*a noise like thunder*'. Yesterday your poor history teacher, Miss Ping, actually fainted in the classroom at the pong and had to be taken to the sickbay."

"I think Ping did the pong," suggested Mindy with another smirk.

"It's *Miss* Ping and, for your information, in the twenty years she has worked at this school I have never known the fragrant Miss Ping to make a pong. Now what do you have to say for yourself?"

An evil thought shot across the girl's mind.

PPPFFFTTT! came a sound.

There was a short delay as the pongtastic aroma floated across the room. Finally the dark and dirty **SMELL** snaked its way up the headmistress's nostrils. The lady hastily covered her mouth and nose with her handkerchief.

"You wicked child!" she shouted as *Windy Mindy* stifled a giggle. "Get out! Get out of my office at once!"

She shooed the little girl out of the room as quickly as she could. "Shoo! Shoo! SHOO!"

As Mindy took each step towards the door, she blew a little *bottom bubble* in the direction of the lady.

PFT!

PFT!

PFT!

PFT!

"One more sound out of you and you will be expelled! Do you hear me?

EXPELLED!"

bellowed the headmistress and slammed her office door shut.

BANG!

Mindy stood alone in the corridor once more. Feeling rather pleased with herself, she skipped off, *tooting* all the way.

PFT! PFT! PFT! PFT!

Not wishing to return to her maths lesson, Mindy looked for an empty classroom to hide in until break-time. She slipped into the music room. An array of instruments stood ready to be plucked, played or blown into.

Unsurprisingly, Mindy was drawn to the wind instruments. *The saxophone, the trumpet, the trombone, the tuba* all stood glistening on their stands. The biggest of them all was the tuba, and Mindy walked slowly towards it, as if in a trance. The little girl had no musical ability she knew of and when she tried to blow into the instrument, a pathetic rumbling sound came out.

But just as she was about to give up Mindy had a mischievous thought. She held the end of the tuba behind her behind, blowing *wind* from her bottom towards the tuba as

hard as she could.

A long low note came from the tuba.

DOOOOOOOOOOOOOOOOOOOOOOoooooo....

Pleasantly surprised at the sound, Mindy tried again. Three higher notes this time, in quick succession.

DEE DAH! DEE DAH! DEE DAH!

The girl was beginning to get a feel for the instrument now.

Soon Mindy started putting the notes together in something resembling a tune. It wasn't a classical masterpiece; rather it had the feel of free-form JAZZ about it.

DOO DUM DOO DUM DEE DAH DUM! DAH

Delighted at this discovery, Mindy began to whirl round the room with the tuba at her behind. The sound the girl was making by now was nothing short of wondrous.

DOO DUM DOO DUM DEE DAH DUM DOO
DUM DOO DAH DUM DEE DAH DEE DUM DAH DUM!!!

Outside the classroom the elderly music teacher, Mr Tinkle, was passing by. The music stopped him in his tracks. In all his years of teaching, he had never heard a pupil play so superbly. It brought tears to his eyes. When Mr Tinkle opened the door to the music room, so did the *smell*.

At first the music teacher was horrified at what he saw. One of his beloved instruments being powered by a windy child's bottom. He was about to shout at Mindy to stop, but the sheer beauty of the music made him pause. As the music soared, so did his heart. This young girl was a musical **prodigy**. She could become one of the all-time greats, playing huge sell-out concerts all over the world! As for Mr Tinkle, he would be remembered as the humble teacher who discovered a musical superstar.

"Mindy!" he exclaimed. "You are a genius!"

"It's just my bottom burping, sir," replied the little girl.

"I know. But please keep those beautiful *bottom burps* coming. The sound they make is magnificent!"

"If you say so, sir."

That night the music teacher rushed over to **Windy Mindy's** house to talk to her long-suffering parents about his master plan. They were delighted that their daughter's dubious "gift" could at last be put to good use, and even more delighted that it would get her out of the house. Now they wouldn't have to sit watching television with pegs on their noses.

The next morning at school, Mr Tinkle presented the girl with a very special present. A shiny new tuba.

"Now, Mindy," began Mr Tinkle, "I need you to practise, practise, practise until your bum goes numb!"

"Yes, sir!"

"I have booked the greatest music venue in the world to launch your glittering career!

THE ROYAL ALBERT HALL!"

PFT! went the girl's bottom.

"Was that on purpose?" asked the music teacher.

"No, sir, just nerves."

So enthused was Mr Tinkle about his protégée's talents that he set about inviting the greatest composers and conductors from all over the world to her concert debut. He even invited royalty – the Duke and Duchess of *Somewhere or Other*.

Meanwhile Mindy did just as Mr Tinkle said. Every night after school she spent hours in the music room practising on her tuba. There was so much **toxic gas** in the room that the paint peeled off the walls, much to the delight of the little girl. And her big night was FAST approaching...

* * *

Finally the day came. **Windy Mindy** was to make her
world debut at the ROYAL ALBERT HALL.

In Mindy's vast dressing room backstage, there
were some last-minute preparations. The little girl was
delighted to devour as many of her special **windy**
foods as she possibly could.

Porridge beans dried figs mushy peas cauliflower cheese eggs lentil soup Lentil and prune juice PRUNE cabbage stuffing

were all mixed together in a
giant vat before she poured
them down her throat.

To ensure that she would have enough **wind** for the
performance, she topped it off with a
huge bottle of fizzy pop.

Now Mindy's tummy was
bubbling with
air.

"Isn't it great? I think I am going to explode, sir!" she said. "I will have enough *wind* to play for hours," she added, before excitedly clambering on to a trampoline. As soon as she started bouncing up and down, she began counting.

"Three hundred!

Two hundred and ninety-nine!

Two hundred and ninety-eight!"

A tiny *tommy squeaker* escaped from Mindy's bottom with every jump.

BOING!

BOING!

BOING!

After bouncing for over an hour, the food and drink in the girl's tummy had been mixed together nicely, or horribly, depending on how you look at it.

Meanwhile all of the distinguished guests had been seated in the auditorium. Even the Duke and Duchess of *Somewhere or Other* had come, he in a velvet dinner suit, she in a ball gown with a diamond tiara atop her head.

The lights dimmed and a spotlight shone on Mr Tinkle as he shuffled on to the huge stage of the ROYAL ALBERT HALL.

"Your Royal Highnesses, my lords, ladies and gentlemen, welcome to this very special evening. Tonight I am going to introduce to you my **musical** discovery. A girl who just one month ago had never played a note of music in her life!"

There was a gasp from the audience. They could hardly believe their ears.

"Please! Please!" called Mr Tinkle over murmurs that were growing louder by the moment.

"You will not be disappointed. This young girl is one of the greatest free-form JAZZ TUBA players of our age. No – OF ALL **TIME!**"

The audience broke into wild applause. Mr Tinkle smiled and bowed his head before continuing.

"Ladies and gentlemen, I give you...

WINDY MINDY!"

The audience shook their heads in disbelief as the little girl strolled on to the stage. Surely there was some mistake?

This child was far too **SMALL**

to be a great tuba player.

Mindy smiled and bowed to the audience. As she did
so, a little *pop-pop* pop-popped out of her bottom.
Mr Tinkle looked on nervously from the side of the
stage. Fortunately, as it was downstage, no one seemed
to hear, though one of the backstage workers did faint.

Next, Mindy turned round and placed the tuba
behind her **bottom**, ready to blow her *wind*
towards it.

GASP!

The audience were
scandalised. They had
never seen anything so
rude. And in the ROYAL
ALBERT HALL indeed.
Which is not just a big
hall, but is actually *royal*!

For a moment it seemed like a riot might break out. Mindy looked across to Mr Tinkle, who gestured frantically for the girl to begin.

So she did.

Immediately sweet music filled the hall. The audience were shocked into silence. The sound Windy Mindy made was beautiful beyond words. After just a few notes, she had everyone entranced. They were all in the palm of her bottom.

This was a moment in music history that the world would never forget, Mr Tinkle was sure of it.

However...

...after all that **gassy food** and fizzy pop plus, of course, all the bouncing up and down on a trampoline, Mindy's **wind** was particularly fierce.

The **smell** was so appalling it actually **BURNED** the nostrils when it went up the nose.

Needless to say, dear reader, this is the point in the story where things began to go **horribly wrong**.

Suddenly the music teacher noticed that one by one the rows of audience members were withering like dead flowers. First the front row with the Duke and Duchess in it,

then the second,

then the third. The **stink** was hitting them like a tidal wave.

As Mindy played on, she forced more and more gas out of her bottom. In no time at all, the entire audience had passed out.

Mr Tinkle rushed on to the stage to make Mindy stop, but the wall of smell floored him in an instant, and he fell off the stage and plunged into a piano in the orchestra pit.

CLANG!

Suddenly Mindy realised that, as much as she
WANTED to, she just

COULDN'T **STOP** BLOWING OFF.

Up until today she had always enjoyed being able to
deliver her trumps to order.

But now her bottom

was buzzing way out

of control

and her bubbly tummy

was EXPANDING

at an alarming rate.

Nothing

could HOLD

the gas back.

Her

bottom

was about to go

NUCLEAR!

There was an eerie silence for a few seconds before...

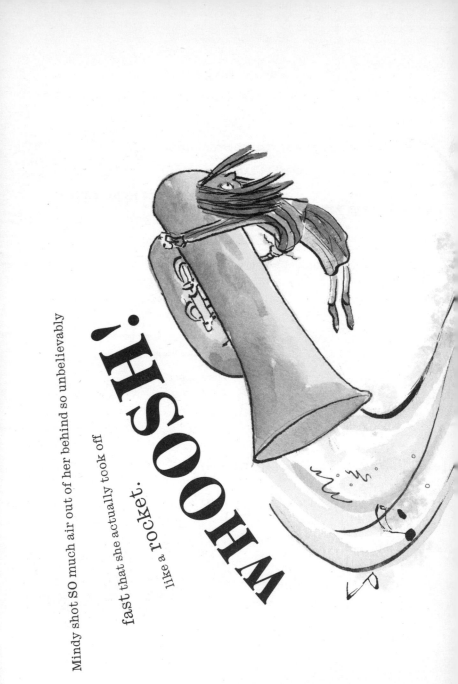

Mindy shot SO much air out of her behind so unbelievably

fast that she actually took off

like a rocket.

WHOOSH!

The gas propelled her and her tuba up, up, up into the air, and she smashed through the domed roof of the ROYAL ALBERT HALL.

CRASH!

Mindy zoomed up through the starlit sky at lightning speed, heading straight for OUTER SPACE.

WHIZZ!

Up there on an **International Space Station**, the astronauts on board reported hearing some rather impressive **free-form JAZZ**. Thinking it might be alien life attempting to make contact, they put on their space suits and rushed outside, only to find themselves gazing open-mouthed in shock at...

a little girl hurtling past

with a tuba behind her behind,

and a look of terrible panic on her face.

That was the very last sighting of **Windy Mindy**.

So what is the moral of this tale, I hear you ask?

It's that there is absolutely

nothing funny about **breaking wind**.

Which is why I would *never* write a story about it.

Earnest
ERNEST

EARNEST ERNEST HAD MADE IT to twelve years old without ONCE cracking a smile. The boy loved to be deadly serious all of the time. He was far too **pompous** to involve himself in anything that might be considered "**FUN**". Joy and laughter were strangers to him. He never watched cartoons or played games or went to birthday parties.

The other children in school would try to include him, but the boy chose to spend all his time alone, immersed in some incredibly boring hobbies.

Ernest had an unrivalled collection of *pencil-sharpenings*

and on weekends he would photograph **traffic lights**, then stick the pictures in a series of scrapbooks labelled *Traffic Lights 1–217*.

However, Ernest's most favourite hobby of all was a guessing game of his own invention, where he would attempt to deduce what types of metal various objects were made of.

"Mother, I do believe that said toaster has been manufactured from the metal *steel*," declared the boy one morning, as he sat in the kitchen with his long-suffering mother. Ernest's clothes were like a uniform. He always wore the same grey lace-up shoes, grey trousers and grey shirt buttoned right up to the collar.

In contrast to **Earnest Ernest**, his mother was a jolly soul. A tall, lively lady who wore brightly coloured clothes with loud flowery patterns. However, her face was increasingly lined with worry about the fact that her son had never laughed or even smiled.

Dutifully she picked up the toaster, and studied the engraving on its underside.

"Correct AGAIN, Ernest!"

she muttered with as much enthusiasm as she could muster.

"Now, Mother, let us move on to said toilet-roll holder. I do believe it has been manufactured from the metal *aluminium*."

"Correct again, Ernest! What a splendid game this is. I **never** tire of it," she lied. Then Mother plucked up the courage to ask a question. "Ernest, I was wondering if you might want to go and do something **FUN** today."

"**FUN?**" Ernest exclaimed.

"Mother, what is this 'FUN' that you speak of?"

"Well, you know... amusement."

"Amusement?"

"Yes. **FUN** could be anything, like... going to the *zoo*. Watching the orang-utans playing together can be very amusing," replied the woman.

"I hardly think so, Mother," stated the boy coldly. "Said orang-utans are merely apes that are orange. What on earth is 'amusing' about that?"

His mother sighed and tried again. "Then we could go to the **fairground**. It's always *funny* looking at yourself in a hall of mirrors."

"Mother, why on earth would that be..." Ernest could barely bring himself to say the word, "**...FUNNY?**"

"Well..." It wasn't easy to describe such a thing to someone with absolutely **no** sense of humour. "Well, you look in one mirror and you are *tall* and *thin!*"

The boy was unmoved. "Pray continue, Mother..."

"And then you... **erm...**"

Ernest stared at his mother, his lip curling in **disdain**.

"...you look in the **next** mirror and, would you believe it, you are *short* and *fat!* **Ha ha ha!**"

Her laughter came to an abrupt halt as Ernest frowned at her with contempt.

"Mother, I am neither tall and thin, nor short and fat. Why cannot the hall of mirrors just be normal mirrors, coated, of course, with the metal *aluminium?*"

"Because, Ernest, then the funny mirrors wouldn't be **FUNNY!**" The woman was exasperated now. "Look, son, please let's just forget the zoo and the fairground because there is something even better."

"Really?"

"YES! I found out this morning there is a CIRCUS in town!"

Ernest's nose wrinkled with scorn, but his mother pressed on regardless.

"We could go and see the clowns. They never fail to make the entire audience *hoot* with laughter!"

"These 'clowns' of which you speak are amusing, are they, Mother?"

"Oh yes, Ernest! Hilarious!" replied the lady in a flash. It seemed she might have hooked the boy at last; now she just had to reel him in.

"They drive into the circus tent in a little clown car and, before they can even get out of the car, the doors fall off! Ha ha ha ha!"

Ernest was lost in thought.

"Mother, what metal is said car made of?"

Mother shook her head. "I don't know, son. That's not really the point."

"Is it the metal *steel?*"

"I don't know. And then the clowns get out of the car and they all have these big buckets of water and—"

"Mother, what metals are said buckets made of?"

"I don't know!"

"Zinc?"

"Ernest, please, for goodness' sake! It's not important what stupid metal the buckets are made of!"

Ernest shot his mother a stare that could kill an elephant. "There is nothing stupid about metal, Mother. Ever since I was two years old, I have been studying it," Ernest continued in his monotonous monotone. "I find its properties fascinating. Did you know, for example, that the chemical symbol for silver is Ag from the Latin word for silver – argentum?"

"Yes, yes, yes, I am sure that is fascinating, but—"

"Correct, Mother, it is fascinating. So it is a resounding no to said offers of visits to said zoo, said fairground or said circus. Now, if you will excuse me, I must get back to my collection of **cheese graters**."

With that he marched out of the kitchen and upstairs to his bedroom.

The walls of Ernest's room were painted grey. The bed was grey, the duvet was grey, the curtains were grey. Sometimes it was hard to spot Ernest in there since his clothes were all grey too.*

*Grey was Ernest's favourite colour because it was the colour of most metals. Except gold, which is gold; and silver, which is silver. Which is a bit like grey. Ernest regarded all colours that were not grey to be "far too colourful".

Up in his bedroom, Ernest spent the remainder of the day studying his **cheese graters**.

Mother was ordered to leave his dinner outside his bedroom on a tray. It was a plate of cold peas. That was all Ernest ever ate for breakfast, lunch and dinner. Bowls or plates of the most boring vegetable in the world.

The next morning Ernest's mother woke more sick with worry than ever before. Her son was twelve years old. Soon he would be a teenager. She was desperate for him to experience all those things children should before it was too late. Joy. Laughter. Fun. Friends.

As she took yet another bag of frozen peas out of the freezer for Ernest's pea-based breakfast, she realised that DRASTIC ACTION WAS NEEDED

IF SHE WAS EVER TO SEE HER BOY SMILE.

So Mother did some research and in a newspaper found the following advertisement:

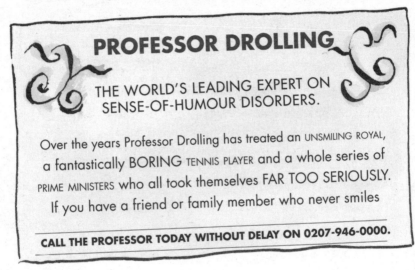

PROFESSOR DROLLING

THE WORLD'S LEADING EXPERT ON SENSE-OF-HUMOUR DISORDERS.

Over the years Professor Drolling has treated an UNSMILING ROYAL, a fantastically BORING TENNIS PLAYER and a whole series of PRIME MINISTERS who all took themselves FAR TOO SERIOUSLY. If you have a friend or family member who never smiles

CALL THE PROFESSOR TODAY WITHOUT DELAY ON 0207-946-0000.

Ernest's mother made an appointment for the very next day.

Professor Drolling's study was situated on the hundredth floor of a hospital. Medical certificates adorned the walls, there was a glass case full of awards and the professor even had a vast oil painting of himself hung behind his desk. This was a man at the absolute **TIP-TOP** of his profession.

As Ernest sat outside in the waiting area, flicking through a copy of *Spoon Monthly,* Mother told the man everything. She told him about her son's **pencil-sharpenings** collection, the diet of cold peas and the scrapbooks of **photographs of traffic lights** that had now reached 558 volumes. Then she told him how Ernest had never, ever laughed or even smiled.

"In all my years in the medical profession, this is by far the most serious case of

NO-SENSE-OF-HUMOUR DISORDER

I have ever heard of!" exclaimed Professor Drolling excitedly. "If I can make your son Ernest smile, I will go down in history as one of the greatest scientists of all time!"

Mother was not convinced he could do it, despite all his expertise. "But how on earth are you going to manage it, Professor? I have tried absolutely everything."

With a theatrical flourish the professor yanked back a long curtain.

"Let me introduce you to my latest invention...

THE Tickle Monster 3000!"

It was a

GIANT ROBOT!

Instead of arms, the robot had a

number of long metal tentacles.

"Oh my!" gasped Ernest's mother.

"Oh my, indeed!" agreed the professor. "My **Tickle Monster 3000** will tickle your boy into helpless gales of laughter in no time. Bring him in, right this instant!"

Mother opened the door of the study. "Ernest, can you come in now, please?"

"But, Mother, I am just reading a fascinating article about the different types of metal used in spoons of all shapes and sizes," he replied without looking up from his magazine.

"I said NOW!" she replied angrily.

Reluctantly the boy put *Spoon Monthly* down and marched into the professor's study.

"A great pleasure to meet you, young Ernest," said Professor Drolling warmly.

The boy simply stood and stared at the man, the usual sour look on his face as if he had swallowed a wasp.

"I know you may think not, but this robot of mine is finally going to make you laugh!"

announced the professor.

"What metal is said robot made of?"
enquired the boy.

"I beg your pardon?" replied the professor,
rather taken aback by the irrelevance
of the question.

"What metal is said robot made of? I am
guessing..." Ernest scrutinised the machine, "...TIN!"

"He does this a lot," muttered Ernest's mother. The
professor sighed and checked the back of his robot.

"You are right!
It is tin.
Well, now we all know that fascinating piece
of information I am going to turn the

Tickle Monster 3000

on in

three,

two,

one..."

With that he flicked a switch on the side and the machine flickered into life. Lights came on and it started to beep.

BEEP! BLEEP! BLOOP!

Next, two of the robot's tentacles stretched out towards the boy.

Ernest tried to run but the grabbers at the end of the tentacles held him still.

"I don't like it!" he complained.

"I promise you, Ernest, it won't hurt," said the professor. He pressed more buttons and two other robot tentacles reached out and started tickling the boy.

The tentacles tickled Ernest in all those places where you are most **ticklesome**.

First under the **chin**,

moving on to the **feet**

and finishing off with the most **dreaded** place of all, the **armpit**.

The professor and the boy's mother studied Ernest's face for even the **flicker** of a smile.

Nothing.

Not even the slightest **suggestion** of one.

"This is most peculiar. Most peculiar indeed. Let me turn up the power!" declared the professor.

On the robot's chest was a dial that read "TICKLE POWER". As the professor turned it, the arrow went from number THREE to number NINE.

Beyond that was TEN, and beyond that a patch of red labelled "DANGER LEVEL".

The tentacles were now moving with much greater haste than before. What's more, they were darting all over the boy's body, finding new places to tickle.

His *knees.* His *tummy.* Even his *ears.*

All felt the full force of Professor Drolling's invention.

Again he and the boy's mother studied Ernest's face.

Again, nothing.

"Mother, can we go home now so I can play with my collection of IRON FILINGS?"

But before the lady could answer the professor shouted, "NO!"

He shouted so loudly that it made Mother jump.
"Ooh!" she cried.

Then, with a whip of his wrist, the professor spun the
dial on his robot to **"DANGER LEVEL"**.

"Are you sure this is safe?" said
Ernest's mother, a look of panic
shooting across her face.

"I don't know," replied the professor,

"but I will get this blasted boy

of yours to LAUGH, if it is the last thing I do!"

The **Tickle Monster 3000** was now *shaking*
and rattling wildly. More tentacles were shooting
out of its chest, and they began tickling the most
unlikely places on Ernest's body.

His *elbows*. His *nose*. Even his *eyebrows*. Still nothing.

"Mother! This is tiresome in the extreme!"
complained Ernest.

Professor Drolling's face contorted with fury.

"Tickle Monster 3000!" he shouted. "YOU ARE MY LIFE'S WORK! MY GREATEST INVENTION! BUT YOU HAVE FAILED ME!"

With that he took off his shoe and began banging the robot on the head with it.

CLANG! CLANG! CLANG!

The robot *beeped* and hissed.

BLEEP! BLOOP! HISS!

Although it was a machine, it actually sounded angry. It stopped tickling Ernest, and slowly turned to face its master. Then its tentacles stretched out to tickle the professor instead. In no time, they were all over the man's body.

Behind his *ears*.

His *tummy*.

The undersides of his *feet*.

"Ha ha! NO! NO!" cried Professor Drolling. "I hate being... Ha ha ha ha! TICKLED!" The man's body was shaking with laughter.

"Ha ha ha ha ha ha ha ha ha!"

However, this wasn't *joyful* laughter. It was agonised laughter. Being tickled like this was torture. Especially with the **Tickle Monster 3000** on FULL!

"Ha ha ha ha ha ha! HELP! HELP!

PLEASE, SOMEONE **HELP!**"

Mother had to do something. And fast.

In desperation, she made a lunge for the dial on the robot's chest. But the **Tickle Monster 3000** turned its tentacles on her too. Soon Ernest's mother was flat on the floor, her arms and legs flapping, like a beetle stuck on its back.

"Ha ha ha ha ha!"
she wailed.

Meanwhile the robot's movements were becoming increasingly jerky and unpredictable. It was making even more *beeping* and *buzzing* noises.

BING!

BLOOP!

BING!

BING!

BLEEP!

BING!

Soon sparks were flying out of its eyes; smoke was billowing from its head.

The robot's tickling tentacles were now moving so fast they were becoming a blur.

"NO! HA HA! NO!" cried Professor Drolling as tentacles tickled every conceivable part of his body.

"I THINK I AM GOING TO WET MYSELF!"

Trying desperately to escape from his own creation, he wrestled the robot, biting its tentacles. But the machine had him pinned against the wall.

"Ha ha ha ha! NO! NO! NO!

A BIT OF WEE HAS COME OUT!

Ha ha ha ha ha!

I CAN'T TAKE IT

ANY MORE!"

With that, the professor leaped OUT of the window.
As his study was on the hundredth floor of the
hospital, he fell for long enough to shout,

"OH, THAT'S MUCH
BETTER!"

before landing upside down
in a flower bed,
his head buried in
the soil, his legs
waggling in the air.

OW!

Inside the study, **Earnest Ernest** exploded
into helpless laughter.

"Ha ha ha ha ha ha ha ha ha ha ha

Tears were even rolling down the boy's cheeks
and his face had turned pink with joy.

ha ha ha ha ha ha
ha ha ha ha ha ha ha
ha ha ha
ha!"

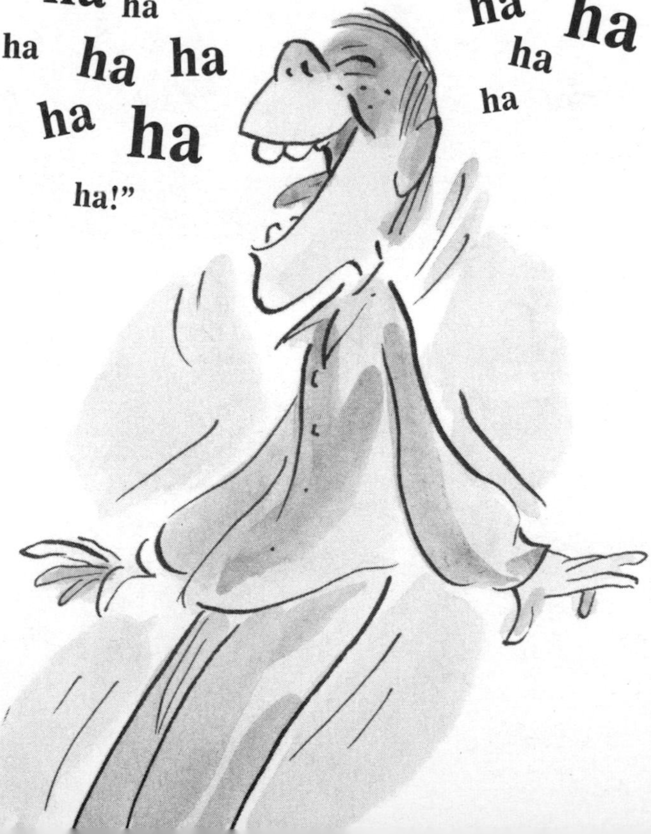

At that moment the **Tickle Monster 3000** finally broke down and keeled over. It hit the floor with a loud...

CLUNK!

"Ernest. You are laughing.
        You are finally laughing!
But why?" demanded his shocked mother.

"Because THAT was funny!" replied Ernest.

So you see, Ernest was not so earnest after all.
He could smile and even laugh, but sadly only
at the grave MISFORTUNE of others.

The boy's poor mother never, ever tried to
make her son laugh again.

As for Ernest, when he grew up, he found his perfect job. He became a science teacher. Ernest worked at the same school for forty years and none of the teachers or pupils ever saw him laugh. He bored everyone day in and day out with his bum-numbing seriousness.

Until one day an experiment went badly wrong in his classroom and there was a massive explosion.

BOOM!

Flames flew and his poor lab technician's bottom caught fire. All the pupils looked on in shock as their teacher hooted with laughter.

"Ha ha ha ha!" snorted Ernest, pointing at the smouldering assistant.

In fact, he hooted so hard that a little bit of WEE came out. It ran down Ernest's trouser leg and formed a puddle on the classroom floor.

And at that moment the whole class laughed at him.
Suddenly **Earnest Ernest** didn't
see the funny side at all.

SOFIA
Sofa

ALL SOFIA WANTED TO DO was sit on the sofa all day, watching television. **Sofia Sofa** was without doubt one of the absolute worst children in the world.

She never went to school, or helped her mum with chores around the house, or even got up to have dinner at the dining table. All she did was sit and watch TV.

It didn't matter what was on: soap operas, GAME SHOWS, detective shows, gardening programmes, talent shows, CARTOONS, POLITICAL PROGRAMMES, even shows about old boring junk that the presenter pretended were priceless ANTIQUES. As long as the screen was flickering, Sofia was glued to it. Adverts were her absolute favourite. Sometimes she felt that the programmes got in the way of the adverts.

All day and all night Sofia would sit slumped on the sofa in front of the TV, eating and watching.

Crisps, biscuits, cake, sweets and chocolate were her favourite foods to gobble as she watched. If an advert came on for crisps, biscuits, cake, sweets or chocolate then she would shout out to her mum to bring her more.

"M-U-V-V-E-R!" she would yell. "CHOCOLATE – NOW!"

The girl's poor mum (she was poor because she had to spend all her money on colossal amounts of food for her daughter) would have to dash out to the corner shop to buy Sofia a bar of chocolate.

However, by the time the woman returned home, Sofia would have seen another advert for something else she wanted to scoff and she'd send her mum straight back out the door again.

"M-U-V-V-E-R! CAKE!"

Watching and eating. Eating and watching. That is all Sofia did. Her eyes had actually become square from staring at the box all day. The only exercise Sofia took was changing channels on the television. But because she had a remote control this was nothing more than pressing a button with her finger. Still, sometimes her finger would get tired and she would shout out to her mum, **"M-U-V-V-E-R! CHANNEL THREE. NOW!"**

It will come as no surprise to you that one day Sofia's mum decided enough was enough.

"It's time you stopped watching television and got off your bottom for once, young lady!" commanded the woman.

"Nah, Muvver," muttered Sofia, not looking up from the television. "I just gotta find out what happens at the end of this programme *fingy*."

"What do you mean, Sofia? The end of the episode?" asked Mum.

"Nah, the end of the series," replied **Sofia Sofa**.

"There is no end! You are watching a soap opera! It will go on FOREVER! Come on, young lady! UP!"

With that Mum put her hands under her daughter's armpits and attempted to hoist her upwards.

"Three, two, one... HEAVE!"

Eventually she managed it, but the sofa came with Sofia.

The girl had been sitting there for so long she had become completely wedged in! In fact the two had somehow fused and it was impossible to tell where the girl ended and the piece of furniture began. Sofia had become...

...half *girl*, half *sofa*.

Not that she was bothered. The girl just carried on staring at the television throughout the whole process.

When Dad returned home from work, Mum enlisted his help. Together the pair of them tried to prise their daughter from the sofa.

Dad put a foot up on one arm of the sofa to create leverage and directed his wife to do the same.

"Three, two, one...

HEAVE!"

But the girl simply would not budge. So Sofia's parents called upon the neighbours in their street of terraced houses to help. The plan was to create a *human chain*. The combined strength of a hundred people would surely separate Sofia from the sofa.

Some folk huddled inside the living room while many others lined up behind them outside.

"GET OUT OF THE WAY OF THE TV!" shouted Sofia.

Dad was at the front, with his arms wrapped round his daughter. Mum held on to him. Indira from next door held on to her and so on.

Arms

linked

as the

human chain

stretched all the way

down the street.

"Three, two, one...

HEAVE!"

called out Dad.

But still the girl wouldn't budge an inch. Sofia's dad fell backwards and the neighbours toppled over each other like dominoes and ended up lying in a big heap, some of them in front of Sofia.

"YOU'RE STILL BLOCKIN' THE TV!" she moaned.

There was nothing else for it. Dad decided to call the EMERGENCY SERVICES.

"What service do you require?" said the operator. "POLICE, FIRE or AMBULANCE?"

"I am not sure," began Dad as Mum looked on anxiously. "You see, my daughter has become attached to a sofa."

"As in she likes it a lot?" enquired the operator.

"No, as in they are joined together," answered Sofia's dad.

"Oh dear. That is an unusual one," replied the operator. "We had a man the other day whose BOTTOM had become JAMMED in a bucket, and a lady whose HEAD had become LODGED in a melon, but we have never had anyone WEDGED in a SOFA. I COULD SEND THE FIRE BRIGADE TO CUT HER OUT."

"That seems a bit drastic," said Dad.

"KEEP IT DOWN! I IS WATCHIN' TV!"

shouted Sofia.

"What was that?" asked the operator.

"Nothing," whispered Dad.

"Just my lovely daughter, the one who is half girl, half sofa."

"Oh." The operator thought for a moment. "I could send the police to arrest somebody?"

"Who?" asked Dad.

"The sofa?"

Sofia's dad pondered this. "No... The sofa hasn't done anything wrong and we rather like it."

Mum nodded her head in agreement.

"How about an ambulance? They can take your daughter to the hospital and perhaps a surgeon can perform an operation to separate her from the sofa?"

"Yes, yes, that's a super idea," replied Dad. "Please send an ambulance right away! Thank you."

NEE-NAW NEE-NAW NEE-NAW!

The ambulance arrived in minutes.

But there was a problem.

Being half *girl*, half *sofa*, **Sofia Sofa** was too large to fit through the front door.

So the ambulance driver called for a crane with a giant wrecking ball to help.

Less than an hour later the giant crane swung its heavy metal ball at the front of Sofia's terraced house.

BASH!

The wall was smashed to pieces. As a cloud of dust enveloped everyone in the street, still Sofia sat watching her beloved television.

"GET THAT DUST OUT OF ME WAY NOW! I CAN'T SEE THE TV!" she shouted.

When the dust cleared, the ambulance driver found there was another problem. The half *girl*, half *sofa* was too heavy to lift. So the ball was taken off the crane's chain, and the chain was secured round the bottom of the sofa.

With a pull of a lever...

WHOOSH!

...the half *girl*, half *sofa* was hoisted high up into the air.

When Sofia could no longer see her beloved television, she started making an awful racket.

"TV! TV! TV!"

she chanted.

The crane operator panicked and pulled the wrong lever, sending his load swinging through the air. It smashed into the row of houses on the other side of the road. CRASH! The houses came tumbling down in an explosion of dust and debris. BOOM!

There wasn't much of the terraced street left.

Not that Sofia cared; all she cared about was watching television.

When the noise of falling brickwork and the screams of innocent bystanders had subsided, all that could be heard was the girl chanting loudly,

"TV! TV! TV! TV! TV! TV!"

As quickly as she could, the ambulance driver opened the back doors of her vehicle. The crane driver attempted to swing the half *girl*, half *sofa* inside. After around five hundred tries it became clear it was not going to fit. So the ambulance driver had an idea. Using a rope she secured the half *girl*, half *sofa* to the rear of her ambulance so she could pull **Sofia Sofa** all the way to the hospital.

"TV! TV! TV! TV! TV! TV! TV! TV! TV!"
came the chant.

By now the driver was so desperate to stop this ear-torturing noise, she was willing to try anything. So she plugged the television into the back of the ambulance.

It flickered to life once more in front of Sofia. That was the longest she had gone without watching television since she could remember. The TV had been off for a whole minute, and she was relieved it was back on again.

The ambulance driver drove off as slowly and gently as possible. The girl's parents sat upfront in the cab as their daughter and the television trailed behind.

The half *girl*, half *sofa* seemed happy enough as she trundled along in the direction of the hospital. After all she could watch TV for the entire journey.

And all went well until...

The ambulance took a sharp corner...

SCREECH!

...and both the rope and the

electricity cable on the TV snapped.

THWACK!

The ambulance driver sped on unaware, but the television and half *girl*, half *sofa* flew across the road untethered.

ZOOM!

As the television was now unplugged, the screen went black.

Sofia began chanting wildly.

"TV! TV! TV! TV! TV! TV!"

But, as luck would have it, at that very moment...

the half *girl*, half *sofa* bashed straight through
the window of a television shop.

SMASH!

Sofia Sofa flew through the air and landed…

...inside a giant-screen television.

SHATTER!

Instantly she became wedged within.

Now **Sofia Sofa-Television** was one-third *girl*, one-third *sofa* and one-third *television*.

Which is exactly what can happen
if you watch too much **TV**.